RIVERS
AND ROADS

Alicia M. Bynum

J P

**Jan-Carol
Publishing, Inc**

"every story needs a book"

Rivers and Roads
Alicia M. Bynum

Published October 2025
Mountain Girl Press
Imprint of Jan-Carol Publishing, Inc
All rights reserved
Copyright © 2025 by Alicia M. Bynum

ISBN: 978-1-970471-09-0 (Paperback)
ISBN: 978-1-970471-10-6 (Hardcover)
Library of Congress Control Number: On file

You may contact the publisher:
Jan-Carol Publishing, Inc
PO Box 701
Johnson City, TN 37605
publisher@jancarolpublishing.com
www.jancarolpublishing.com

Dedicated to Grandpa and Grandma,
for showing me life through the lens of travel.

And to Mammaw and Pappaw,
for raising me a true Appalachian.

To Mom and Dad, I'm lucky to be your daughter,
and I love you both more than words.

And to my daughter,
who holds the key to the future.

In memory of the Nolichucky River and to her recovery.

RIVERS AND ROADS

Contents

"Eastward I go only by force,
but Westward, Westward I go free."

— Hearsay from the Oregon Trail

1

Visitor

The summer of 2015, my mother rode nine hours as my passenger to Gulf Breeze, Florida. This was no vacation, and my intentions were ill much like her state of mental health.

I sat across from the lawyer beside my Aunt Nora, my mother's eldest sister, a few weeks before the drive south. After multiple dealings with the police and state of Tennessee rehabilitation centers, my aunt and I decided it was necessary to pursue an external source for the safety of my mother. Her mental health was steadily declining. Though we could see clear as stained glass that Mom was sick, the illness created a false reality for her. She refused to believe that she needed help. The lawyer listened, as we attempted to explain our story without sounding crazy ourselves.

"And then, the police had us removed from my grandfather's property for trying to get Mom help," I told him.

He wrote everything down in a wide-ruled notebook and studied it for quite a while before consulting us. Nora and I sat quietly in our own muse of disbelief and confusion. There was never a single moment when we felt confident in how to care for my mother. We were exhausted from losing relationships with those who cared about us in efforts to free my mother from her own mind. The lawyer returned from the privacy of closed doors with a semi-blank expression on his face.

He asked, "Are either of you familiar with obtaining a Power of Attorney?"

I felt my palms grow clammy and my stomach ache. Nora explained to him that we were hoping for other options. My mother had been committed to the local mental hospital a total of four times since I was born. I never understood it when I was younger.

My mammaw once said, "Millie, run along and play outside. Your mom isn't feeling well."

I remember seeing Mom sitting there rocking back and forth on the couch speaking a language I didn't understand. She couldn't remember her name or what year it was. I followed Mammaw's advice and went to climb the tree in her front yard. Mammaw always knew what was best. In a few days, Mom was back to *normal*. My mammaw was the glue that held our family together over the decades. She died in the summer of 2012, and we were all torn for direction.

I remember stringing beans that we'd pick from the garden one evening.

Mammaw said, "She used to be the light of every room she walked in, Millie. I don't know what's happened to her."

I didn't know what she meant then, but Mom was becoming increasingly paranoid. I always thought of my mom as carefree, adventurous, and resilient. As I grew older, I realized that she was changing, though she still looked and sounded the same. After my mammaw passed away, Mom jumped the final stretch to the deep end. All at once, she stopped fighting the demons in her head and let them move in free of rent.

The lawyer suggested we get a court order for my mother's Power of Attorney. She refused to take her medication regularly, and her diagnosis had become a mixed bag. The lawyer left us in the cold room to talk privately.

My aunt said, "Millie, I love her, but I can't do it. I've spent so much of my time down there trying to help her, and I'm so tired."

I saw the truth in her eyes. She was mentally drained from trying to fix my mother. It broke her in a way and took a piece of her that would never return. Mom was her younger sister, and Nora had watched her mind deteriorate more vividly than anyone else.

As I entered my early 20s, Mom had become my responsibility. *I could get her POA and force feed her daily prescription drugs, watch her every move, confiscate her keys, get her license revoked, and keep her from harm's way,* I thought inside the lawyer's office. My heart raced. I was not ready for that big of a commitment and knew the stress it would induce. Guilt flooded my veins, and I fought back tears.

"Nora, I don't think I can handle her alone," I said.

I felt selfish. I had dropped out of college twice already, often worrying about her between classes. I knew I wasn't strong enough to become her full-time caregiver.

The lawyer returned. We stayed another hour searching for answers in a room with no meaningful pictures on the wall. It seemed like we were always searching for answers. He estimated startup court costs to *get the ball rolling* at around $8,000. Hell, even if I was onboard, I couldn't afford it. I could barely pay my own rent. Obtaining a POA of a person was serious business. After an upfront large sum of money, Mom would then be summoned to court. He said the summons would have both mine and Nora's names on it. Right then, we made eye contact *terrified.*

"That would never fly," said Nora.

"She's right. Mom would call us every name in the book and more than likely get ill if we tried to force her into a car or something," I said. *Then, how would I convince her to take her meds and ride with me to doctor's appointments once I'd lost her trust?* Tension overcame my neck and back.

"I can't do this!" I panicked.

"Me either," Nora agreed.

We were left as confused as when we first walked in. We walked out of the appointment feeling defeated. A remedy for my mother's mental health was hopeless. Nora offered to supply part of the court fees if I wanted to pursue the POA further. I didn't have the energy nor patience to become Mom's full-time caregiver, especially without her compliance. I wanted to go back to school, travel, maybe have kids and a family one day. It tore me apart watching her health decline. Her medications seemed to worsen the illness more than help, but I was never certain of anything when it came to my mother. I knew it would be a daily battle to convince her to swallow those pills, and I didn't trust them to begin with.

I often have flashbacks to when Mom first began acting *off*. When I was in my senior year of high school, she'd walk outside and stare for hours pointing up to the sky. I think it was Venus or some planet she would obsess over. She called it her "Eye in the Sky" and said it followed her throughout the night. I'd just thought she was being more goofy than usual. She always had a light-hearted approach to life and carried a smile through hardships.

One evening after making dinner, she pulled out a bunch of her medical records and slung them across the table. She told me if they ever tried to commit her to the mental hospital to make sure to give those papers to the doctor. I wasn't really sure what she'd meant. I didn't know who "they" were or why they would commit her. I skimmed over the papers and saw records of a bladder treatment she was receiving every six months for *Interstitial Cystitis*. I remember her feeling so much better after receiving those treatments. That was when she had health insurance.

My dad and I often wondered if Mom's kidney problems affected her mental offset. We were deferred from speaking with her doctors due to HIPAA Privacy Laws and Mom's mule-like desire to keep everything to herself. I was never allowed to speak with her doctors and encourage them to look at her health history of kidney poisoning for a possible contributor to her mental health decline. Maybe I was full of false hope that her mental illness could be reversed. I could only hope that her healthcare providers were studying the depth of Mom's health records and taking all of her diagnoses into consideration when they'd send her home with a jumble of medications.

It was exhausting trying to convince my mother to let me accompany her to doctor's appointments and prying to speak with her healthcare providers. In the meantime, they continued to feed her a mixture of prescription drugs and trusted her in an unstable mental state to properly administer them to herself each day. After Mammaw passed away, my family grew fed up and confused with Mom. They were not around her every day to understand the timeline of her mental decline. It didn't happen overnight, though sometimes it felt like it had. My extended family accused Mom of being on drugs, but I knew her better.

More often, her mental health seemed to be getting worse. The times she was committed to the mental hospital did no good for her. There was a maximum stay of 14 days. They'd release her on the 14th day, for better or worse. One time, they sat her out on the sidewalk, intoxicated with prescription drugs and no ride home. Coincidentally, I was driving over to visit her and passed her walking down the street with her thumb up. She didn't appear any more rational in conversation, rather doped up and numb from the meds. She could barely hold her head up straight and walked like a zombie. A couple days after the meds wore off, she was talking about the president flying over her head in a spaceship and meteorites raining down with healing metals, again. I thought the doctors made her condition worse sometimes.

I received a call one dark morning at 3:00 a.m.

"Millie, come get me. My car is stuck up in a ditch," she said. I was expected to be at work in five hours.

"Are you okay?" I asked, feeling panic seep through my veins.

She said she just needed a ride. I left my dog, Moe, with my roommate and drove the hour out to find her. It was cold and dark, as I searched for my mother down the winding back roads of Washington County. Yet, there she was, standing out in the night with her silver car nose down in a ditch just like she'd said. The back wheels were straight up in the air, and there wasn't a scratch on her. It was a miracle. I asked her what she'd been doing out so late.

"The wind. It led me here," she said.

The sight of her car shook me. I didn't know how she was still alive. I called a 24-hour mechanic, and they towed her car back to my grandfather's house where she resided at the time.

A couple weeks later, my roommate was evicted from our house, and her name was on the lease. So, I packed all my things into my truck bed and drove down to my grandfather's house, hoping to spend a few nights until I could find a new rental to move into.

I drove my truck up the long, familiar driveway between tall rows of pine trees and walked inside. Mom was having one of those days and talking in a circle of concoctions: aliens, solar panels, meteorites, the president, and her *Eye in the Sky*. I dropped my duffle bag on the floor and asked if I could stay a few days until I found somewhere else. She said that it was fine, and her attitude snapped within a matter of seconds.

"Why are you doing this to me?" she asked.

"Doing what? Are you okay?" I asked back.

She shoved me against the white paneled wall and looked deeper into my eyes.

"Why are they doing this to me, Millie?" she asked.

I had a flashback. *Mammaw was sitting in her spot on the couch where she always sat, closest to the hallway.* Days of our Lives *was on the TV. I came running inside after climbing the tree in the front yard. I walked through the kitchen into the hallway and put one palm on each side of the brown paneled wall. I spider monkeyed my way to the top and smacked the ceiling to pin my victory. "Mammaw, come look at what I can do!" I said. She came into the hallway, laughing contagiously, and said, "I need to paint these walls white."*

I pushed Mom off me, and she grabbed my throat and shoved me back against the wall. Her eyes were glazed over, and I couldn't recognize her. I had locked Moe in the bathroom to let him eat and drink some water. She released her grasp on me and flung the bathroom door open.

"Get out of here!" she yelled at Moe and kicked him in the stomach. "He can't be in here!" she yelled.

"Leave him alone!" I yelled back.

Moe took off running to get outside, and Mom chased after him. I ran ahead of her and opened my truck door for him to jump in. I ran back into the house to get my duffle bag and could sense her right behind me. Just as I grabbed my things, she pushed me down to the bed.

"You are going to get me kicked out of here for having that damn dog!" she said, as she kicked my lower abdomen.

My grandfather walked in and told her to stop. I grabbed my duffle bag and ran back to my truck, pulling out of that driveway like a bat out of hell. I didn't

speak to her for six months. I moved into an apartment with my boyfriend and never told her where we lived.

One night, I answered a phone call from an unknown number, and my heart sank as I heard her voice, "Millie?" She'd gotten my number from a family member and called to tell me she'd broken her ankle. It was just after midnight, as she explained to me that the mob had been chasing her. She said a car had flashed its high beams into her eyes and tried to run her over.

"They are out to get me, Millie," she said.

She suspected it was the mafia or our own American government. I shrugged and felt numb to these types of responses. I wanted to believe her, and sometimes I started to. I feared she was getting closer to something really bad happening.

Sometimes, I'd stay awake at night dreading a call that she'd died or killed someone else recklessly driving. I called Nora to vent, and she asked to see me. We met for lunch the next day, and it was unfortunate that all we ever had time to talk about was my mother's mental state. I was so thankful for Nora. We agreed to intervene, again, and told Mom that we had to take her to the hospital as soon as possible to have her ankle X-rayed. While this was semi-true, we knew that tricking her into going to the hospital was one of the only ways to have a mental evaluation performed in the state of Tennessee. It felt dirty. The last thing I wanted was to lose her trust, but I was more scared of losing her life.

We coaxed her into the car from my grandfather's house. On the ride to the hospital, she kept saying, "This is just for an X-ray, right?" She had a keen sense about her still. We arrived at the Emergency Room, and they X-rayed her ankle. There was a deep fracture in the bone. She told the doctor the same story she told us, that the mob was hunting her down.

My aunt stepped outside of the hospital room to speak privately with the doctor about getting Mom a mental health evaluation. This was the first time I'd ever been present for one of her mental evals. It wasn't Nora's first rodeo. I leaned my back onto the wall and slid down to a sitting position on the floor. My skin crawled, and I could feel my heart beating through my ears. I didn't want Mom to get committed, but I was afraid she'd hurt herself or someone else.

Several hours later, the mental health examiner walked in and evaluated my mother on the hospital bed. The woman asked her questions like "What month were you born?" and "What year is it?" Mom couldn't answer any of them clearly, and then she realized why we had taken her there to the hospital. She insulted the healthcare professionals and looked directly into my eyes.

"How could you do this to me, Millie?" she asked.

I wanted to say that I was sorry and didn't know what else to do, but I was speechless and scared of what would happen to her next. I was choking on the silence. My aunt hugged me tightly, as two strong men came into the room and picked Mom up off the bed. They forced her to sit in a wheelchair and held her down against her will as she screamed, "No, no!" She begged me to save her, and I didn't know how.

We followed them out the back doors of the hospital where an unmarked white van was parked and still running. The two men pushed her into the arms of strangers inside of that van, as she screamed and cried. I began to sob and wrapped my arms around my aunt. The van pulled away, and I was left feeling empty with regret. I stayed up all morning, confused and sleep deprived, watching the clock on my phone. I hardly even noticed my boyfriend, who was asleep beside me.

My aunt and I began visitations with my mother at the mental hospital every Wednesday following that awful night. The visits were allotted for one hour per week. Nora and I would meet in the parking lot and walk in together. We'd sit at a table by a vending machine in the lunchroom, where men in blue scrubs guided the patients in. Mom acted glad to see us at first. Then, she began to tell us horrible things. She said that male nurses pulled her out of her showers while she was completely naked and gawked at her in that facility. I never knew whether to believe her or not. I was unsure of how she was treated in those types of facilities and hoped to God for the best.

2

Bonfires

When I was a kid, Mom would take me to the park to play basketball. Nothing else mattered when we were on the court. It was just us and the goal. She had a great shot and even better defense. I'd lose my breath trying to keep up with her, and she inspired me to play harder. We practiced relentlessly on my foul shots to where I rarely ever missed them in games. She'd always be there, cheering me on from the old wooden stands of my elementary school gym. After playing ball, we'd swing by the Dairy Queen for Oreo Blizzards and end the night watching *Friends*.

I had to dig deep for memories like those. All the good stuff we did growing up was being replaced by who my mother was becoming. It was hard to remember who she was deep down and the close relationship we had in the past.

Several weeks passed, and her health did not improve. My boyfriend moved to Colorado to train as a raft guide. I wanted to go but couldn't leave Mom like that in Tennessee. Relationships would come and go, and I felt a need to be near her even though I was unsure how to protect her.

Interactions with my mother left me confused with my own reality. The Appalachian Mountains became a crutch for holding onto my sanity. I took Moe hiking just about every week to familiar waterfalls and Blue Ridge vistas, always searching for new trails to keep my mind fresh. He was the best trail buddy and was always eager to hop through creeks and explore new mountains with me.

I moved out of my apartment and began leasing a house with two great friends I'd known since high school, Jack Gilly and Jack Booker. I had a handful of friends with the name Jack, so I called them all by their last names. We partied together during those days. It helped me not to think about Mom so much, and I was competitively good at beer pong which reminded me of our basketball times together.

Our house in Johnson City was cozy and not too far from where I worked at a local Suboxone clinic. I made $15 per hour, which was pretty good pay back then, especially for Johnson City. At our house, there was a one-sided white picket fence in the front yard and a large, fenced-in backyard. I decided to adopt another dog. I brought Luna home from Piney Flats and introduced her to Moe. They bonded like yin and yang, and I couldn't have imagined life without them.

I started dating Gavin, who I'd known since high school. He was a year younger than me, and we'd dated on and off throughout the years. He introduced me to smoking weed, and we had lots of deep, hazy conversations about life out on the back deck. Too often, I had let myself drown in self-pity worrying about Mom, and Gavin reminded me to set boundaries with her.

I was working as a lab assistant at the clinic. Early on, I felt that I was serving a good purpose in that position. However, as I got to know the doctors better, I realized it was all about money. I spent my downtime between patients Googling places around the world I wanted to travel to. Many of our patients were treated as dollar signs, and after a year, I realized I was caught up playing for the wrong team. I began researching the prescription drug *Suboxone* and didn't feel aligned with the industry I was in.

Sitting in the lab one day, I booked a roundtrip flight to Denver, Colorado. I'd always wanted to see the Rockies and found a round-trip flight for $200. I made a post on social media out of excitement, and two close friends decided to join me. I hadn't been talking to Mom much and thought a trip somewhere new sounded refreshing. Gavin offered to dog sit while I was away.

My two gal pals and I met up with our friend, Mako, in Denver. We took a special-brownie-ride through the Rockies. It was my first time seeing those

Colorado Rockies, and boy, were they something! We drove around through Rocky Mountain National Park, surrounded by beautiful, snowy mountain peaks. We rented snowshoes and hiked to Bear Lake. The snow was waist deep, and I couldn't contain my excitement. Snow was my favorite! I rolled around in it and threw snowballs at Mako. He was fun to mess with. Then, he pegged our friend, Kai, on the back of her head with an ice ball, by accident, and I thought she was going to kill him. But at the same time, it was hilarious. I piggybacked Kai around downtown Aspen, in pure bliss, and we came across a Mary Oliver statue. It read:

Tell me, what else should I have done?
Doesn't everything die at last, and too soon?
Tell me, what is it you plan to do
With your one wild and precious life?
— Mary Oliver

We snowboarded at Vail Mountain, and it was my first time boarding out West. It was super crowded that day, and all the snow was packed down. Still, it was exhilarating and huge mountain riding compared to back East. I came home on a Rocky Mountain high. Exploring new mountain ranges full of hidden trails and wonders had reignited a fire inside, one I'd long kept to ashes. Going home to Tennessee, I'd caught the travel bug.

Upon coming home and returning to work, I was requested by one of the doctors to observe a male patient for a urine drug screen without another lab assistant present. The patient openly expressed a history of sexual assault and requested a male lab assistant. Our clinic doctor insisted we "get on with it" and told me if I didn't observe the patient's urine drug screen, my job was on the line. I walked out and immediately called my supervisor, whose office was based out of state in the Midwest. Later that week, my supervisor spoke with the doctor to work out a severance package for my exit. I wasn't inclined to work there at the lab any longer. Without much hesitancy, next I sold my truck and bought a moped to save gas.

Summer was nearing, and I began training as a raft guide on the Nolichucky River to make extra money. It was the perfect combination of time outside in nature and a source of income. Gavin and Booker joined me for raft guide camp, and we'd carpool to the outpost for whitewater training on the Upper Nolichucky Gorge.

The river was a place of adventure, resilience, and solace. It reminded me of Mom, *how she used to be.* Paddling through big whitewater rapids kept my mind free from constant worrying about the decline of her mental health. Plus, she raised me to love the Nolichucky, and it was a place I could belong.

Paddling downstream, I'd get slapped in the face with white-capped rapids with the river. It was a cold and refreshing wakeup call to be present in life. I learned the bends of the Upper Nolichucky with confidence over the weeks to come. Dolly's Hairy Chest, Rooster Tail, and Twin Eddies were landmarks on the upper section of the river and always a welcomed sight. The Nolichucky River was a place that always felt like home in the chaos of life, and it was somewhere I knew I *belonged.*

When I was younger, Mom and I were regulars, swimming along the banks of the Nolichucky River at Chestoa and Big Rock. She was a river rat at heart, and naturally so was I. We're both Pisces. One of my most favorite memories with her was hanging out at Big Rock. We both have wild curly hair, and thinking back, I can feel mine blowing in the wind, my toes wet and sandy standing shin-high in the river, and Mom laughing after splashing river water on her face. She was beaming with light, a smile so contagious, as the bright sun shined upon her dark-tanned skin. Mom always tanned so well, her golden bronze, dark brown tone, and Mammaw said it was because we had a small percentage of Cherokee Indian in our blood.

My father had been living in Florida for the last five years, when my mother's mental health really declined. I kept in touch with him weekly by phone, and he was not thrilled that I had sold my truck for a moped. My father and I have always been close. He'd moved down to Florida to care for my aging grandparents and couldn't fully comprehend the decline of Mom's mental state during his absence. They had split up when I was two years old. I confided to Dad over the phone that I wasn't on a good path in Tennessee. I spent a lot of time barhopping with friends and feeling stuck, *trapped* by Mom's illness. I feared leaving her alone, yet I was weary of getting too close to her. The Appalachian Mountains and the Nolichucky River were home, but the dogs and I had hiked nearly every trail within three hours of where we lived. I craved new scenery, a new environment, and space far away from my mother.

Mom learned of my address where I lived with the boys and began showing up frequently, *unannounced*. One night, she came over at 1:00 a.m. knocking on the door. Gavin got up to answer it, and both of my roommates woke up confused. We all had to be up early the next morning for river guide training. She said that she could hear little girls out singing in the woods across from our house. Then, she called 911, and a police officer showed up on my doorstep. I explained to him that she was mentally ill and that no one was out in the woods. I asked him to escort her back to her car, but she begged to sleep on our couch. Feeling morally confused, I gave in, and Gavin went home. I was worried about her.

After that, my Aunt Nora and I began researching mental health laws in other states. Tennessee was not helping her and ranked poorly for mental healthcare. Florida was ranked in the top 10 states for mental healthcare facilities, thus began the seed of a plan between my aunt and me. My grandpa in Florida, on my dad's side, called to say he wanted to gift me their old Mercury Grand Marquis. He and my dad weren't huge fans of my moped, though I was happy to be commuting around town on a budget. He insisted I come pick up their old car, as they no longer had use for it. I was grateful.

It seemed like an opportunity to get Mom help and for her to be admitted into a hospital down there. I spoke with Nora and asked Gavin if he would drive down south with us and follow me back in the Merc. My aunt wasn't going to go. Gavin agreed to tag along, knowing that it was going to be a very long drive with Mom to the Gulf Coast. My roommates agreed to watch the dogs while we were away.

I felt guilty not disclosing our plan with Mom. We were going to drive her to Florida, pick up the Merc, and find her help. It was like grasping at straws, seeming a last-ditch effort to get her proper mental healthcare. The state of Tennessee wasn't helping, and the system seemed broken. My aunt told me to have my phone ready if I needed to call her at any point for emotional support. I briefly disclosed my plan to Dad, but he was entirely against the idea. He didn't like Mom being subjected to those types of facilities, though he hadn't witnessed how her mental health had declined over the years.

Gavin, Mom, and I packed up and drove over 600 miles to Gulf Breeze. We stayed in Florida for three days. I'd planned to stay longer to visit with my dad and grandparents but wasn't prepared to handle Mom's behavior. We'd met Dad at a gas station, and Mom had called one of their customers a "bitch" for no reason other than the voices in her own head. I guided her back to the car, afraid someone was going to pick a fight with her. She'd never displayed such vulgar antics before the illness took over. Dad scolded her, trying to wake her to her senses, and I saw immediate regret in his face. He was just beginning to see how much the illness had changed her. Mom pushed all of our buttons on that trip, and it was difficult to remember she was sick in those moments of her acting out. This was not the woman who had raised me, and I was ill-equipped on how to care for her.

Jaded memories of Mom slipped to and from my mind as we spent time *trapped* together in Florida. *She bought me my first pair of rollerblades during my 5th grade summer. We would skate down the sidewalk around the back of our old apartment. Mom was flying down the sidewalk, and I was trying to keep up. She was such a good skater and always so tan in the summertime. Her bleached blonde curls were waving behind her, and all of a sudden, she started swatting both hands in the air. It looked like she was from out of a cartoon waving her arms like that, and I finally caught up with her. "Millie, there's a bee! Look out!" she exclaimed. She rolled in place and quickly slipped like there was a banana peel underneath her. She looked up at me, and we heard a group of laughs behind us. There was a neighborhood family cookout, all who had witnessed her bee-dance. We busted out laughing, and I threw out a hand to pull her up. We skated home and tossed an ice pack on her tailbone and relived the story for years to come.*

The plan to trick Mom into the hospital while we were in Florida failed. I didn't have the willpower to follow through without my aunt there. Dad still resisted the idea. He said she didn't belong in a place like that. It all confused me, and I began to question my own motives. I felt immense guilt trying to trick her, but more so I wanted to help her get better and couldn't do it alone. I agreed with Dad to a point, but he hadn't been there to see her mind deteriorate day by day or land her vehicle nose down in that ditch. He hadn't undergone several confrontations with the police over her or had her showing up randomly at his jobs and homes for the past several years. He hadn't witnessed her break her ankle walking around back roads after midnight or lost roommates, relationships, and sanity from her new reality. Not a soul seemed to have any answers on how to help her, and all the while, Nora and I were scared something bad was bound to happen.

My grandfather took me for a ride in the ole Merc, as Gavin hung out with Dad and tested his patience with Mom. This was the car I had ridden in on my first road trip out West, where Grandma and Grandpa introduced me to Wyoming around the age of 12.

I remember seeing dozens of cacti everywhere once we reached the mountainous terrain of Utah. Making our way up to Idaho, right on the Wyoming border, I saw them for the first time. The Grand Tetons. They were the biggest mountains I had ever seen. We met up with my uncles and aunts and picked my dad up at the airport. My uncle guided us down The Snake River. It was the first river I'd ever whitewater rafted in. I sat near the middle of the raft with my cousin, as the adults paddled us through thick class V rapids. My uncle said, "We're approaching the Lunch Counter; brace yourselves!" The raft dipped down through a roller coaster of a rapid, and I felt cold water splash across my face. It was invigorating and would become a staple memory as I got older. My uncle leapt off the boat into the river. Who is guiding us? I wondered. He threw his hand back up onto the raft and said, "Grab these, Millie!" He'd recovered his favorite pair of Oakley sunglasses, and we pulled him back into the raft. I thought, That must have been a special pair of glasses.

Now, here I was in the driver's seat with Grandpa teaching me how to operate all the nooks and crannies. I coasted at a steady 5 MPH through the

Walmart parking lot, and he said, "Whoa, take it easy!" He showed me how to work the cruise control and even left me a couple of his favorite cassettes, including a childhood favorite, *Camp Itchy-Foot*.

"Millie, you have to promise me one thing," he said, "You need to get back into school, and I expect you to make straight As."

I gave him a warm hug and agreed to go back to school *one day*. I'd always loved going to school before everything changed with Mom. On our last night in Florida, Dad suggested I take Mom out for a sailboat ride. I was against the idea at first, because she was driving me crazy talking circles about things that made no sense. Dad and Gavin loaded the boat into the water anyway and convinced me to be her captain. Sailing was such a peaceful pastime. I sucked up my attitude and invited her onto the Sunfish for an evening cruise.

Sailing on the bay off my grandparent's dock in Florida gave me the same feeling as hiking through the Appalachian Mountains and paddling on the Nolichucky River. I was grateful that my father and grandfather taught me how to sail during the summers when I was a kid. It was something I greatly enjoyed, spending time out in the peaceful Escambia Bay, though I was terrified at the thought of sharks and big fish.

We let a relaxing wind guide us out into the middle of the bay. The sun was warm and inviting like it always was on the Gulf. Mom laughed going through the waves, as saltwater splashed her curly hair. For a moment, it felt like the old her. I asked if she was having fun, and she said, "This is the best day of my life, Millie." My heart muddled, as I tried to ignore the reason I had brought her out to Florida. Her good days made it difficult to remember that the illness had taken her hostage and she was lost in her own mind. I saw my mother that evening on the sailboat, the same woman who had Lifetime movie marathons with me and had always made damn sure I had my own room growing up. The sherbet Florida sunset graced Mom's wild blonde curls as they blew across her face, and we shared a moment on the water together, our Pisces souls entwined as mother and daughter.

We sailed downwind back to the dock. As soon as we stepped off the boat, Mom called me a whore and said, "Don't ever do that to me again." I gulped a deep feeling of betrayal in my gut and tucked that memory far into the back of my mind.

Gavin and I packed the car that night and woke up early to head back to Tennessee. I hugged my dad and grandparents, thanking my grandfather for the car. I squeezed my grandmother tight and gave her a big smooch on the cheek. Before I knew it, we were waving goodbye until we were out of sight (an old family tradition) and crossing the Pensacola Bay Bridge. I was thankful Gavin had agreed to come along and follow us home, because I was feeling confused and defeated over Mom.

I asked her not to smoke in the car, because it had never been smoked in before. She called me nasty words, saying I was only there to cause her grief. I found that to be very ironic; however, I was losing energy to keep up with her irrational arguments. I gave in and let her smoke—rather, she did it anyway. I turned up the radio to blare out her continuous need to talk about God knows what. Aliens. The government. The mob. Yellow this, purple that. My brain was turning to mush, and my patience was wearing thin.

She turned the radio off and talked louder about figments of her imagination I did not wish to entertain. I wanted to scream. I pulled over into the far-right lane to make the next exit for gas and regain my self-composure. Gavin was driving directly behind us. I turned the radio back on, and Mom grabbed the steering wheel. She jerked it right, causing me to swerve one tire off the pavement. I looked over at her and said, "That is it!" I got back onto the road and made it to the exit just in time to pull off the interstate. We approached a red light. I stopped the car, and she went straight for the keys in the ignition. I smacked her arm away and gassed it in time for the light to change to green. She cussed at me and threatened to jump out of the car, opening and closing the passenger door. I veered into the first parking lot I saw, which turned out to be a 24-hour Waffle House. She grabbed her purse and stepped out of the car, slamming the door behind her. Gavin parked beside us and went running after her.

I broke down crying and called my aunt. "Millie, this is your chance to get her help. Call the police, now, and explain her situation," she told me. I called them and was able to request a mental health evaluation without first having to get her to the hospital, since we were in the state of Alabama. Until the health-care professionals arrived, we had to keep her from running off and getting lost. She refused to listen to us now, so we kept an eye on her from a distance. She walked into the Waffle House and sat at a table in the back corner, mumbling to herself.

The police arrived within 20 minutes, and I spoke to an officer. The mental health professional followed shortly and walked into the restaurant to evaluate my mother right there at the Alabama Waffle House. I watched from outside, *in a daze.* Two police officers guarded the entrance and exit doors. My mother went from sitting still to frantically trying to run. I was sick to my stomach and kept telling myself this was to help her. The officers blocked her departure and assisted her outside to an ambulance where they strapped her down to a mobile hospital bed. She never made eye contact with Gavin nor me and seemed to argue with the officers until the doors were locked shut. The officers gave us directions to the hospital they were taking her to. Gavin and I followed the ambulance there.

While in the waiting room, a medical professional walked out and called my name. He said my mother could leave but only if Gavin would let her ride with him. I told the doctor that my mother was a danger to have in the vehicle for anyone and that she desperately needed medical help. She asked for us to come into the room, so I went in and told her I loved her. The doctor explained that she would be committed into a nearby psychiatric unit by the state of Ala-bama. It wasn't Florida, but I felt a strange sense of relief thinking she'd get better care outside of Tennessee.

The five-hour drive home felt like 20. I was emotionally exhausted and worried about how my mother would be treated in that facility, so far from her home. I wished she was there riding beside me singing Indigo Girls and Alanis Morissette like we did on road trips when I was younger.

One time, Mom said, "Millie, pack clothes for the night. Let's go on a trip!" I was probably 13 and so excited to see what adventure she had in mind. We drove to South Carolina and stumbled upon a wide-open lake. We made some new friends who told us about a rope swing. Mom volunteered to be the first one to try it out. She had that wild contagious laugh of hers and convinced me to try the rope swing. It was on my bucket list. Anyways, I finally did it after several minutes of convincing and folks cheering along the shoreline. I didn't have quite as much finesse as Mom and somehow bellyflopped off that rope swing face first into the lake. My mouth must have been wide open from laughing or panicking, because I ended up chipping my front tooth. Mom and I laughed 'til we cried...

Those days seemed long gone, and I needed to focus on staying awake for the drive back to Tennessee. It was comforting to know Gavin was following me. We hit Chattanooga and had three hours to go. I knew I wouldn't make it driving that much longer, so I called up some friends who lived nearby in the city. They invited us over without hesitation to crash on their couch. Gavin followed me there but said he wanted to keep driving. Emotionally exhausted, I surrendered and went to bed instantly.

I got up the next morning and pressed forward the last few hours to Johnson City. It was nice to be greeted by my roommates, two of my greatest friends whom I trusted, and to be in good company. I felt safe. The dogs were happy and jumped up to lick my cheeks. Though somewhat relieved to be back to the familiar, I was empty inside, and nothing was tying me down to this town anymore. Gavin didn't talk to me for a few days.

I studied the world map on my shower curtain as hot water trickled down my shoulders and evaporated flashbacks from the trip to Florida. I thought obsessively about leaving to go anywhere else. My lease on the house was month to month, and I'd received a letter stating that I would get a couple hundred dollars a week after being laid off at the lab. It only took a few moments of consideration to leap at the opportunity to leave my hometown.

Gavin came to my house over the next few days, and we broke up. I was at peace with it, or numb to feelings in general at that point, and eager for a change of scenery. He encouraged me to leave Johnson City. He told me to go out and explore the world and not settle until I found a yard with a true white picket fence, painted on both sides. Maybe we were better as friends.

Gavin rode out with me to the house I'd grown up in with my dad, out in Bowmantown. I reminisced of Christmases spent in the old white farmhouse, the train we'd put together around the bottom of our faux Christmas tree, and our garden that was hand-plowed out front. I thought about the times Mom would pick me up on her nights to keep me and how we'd grab dinner on the way to her many apartments. And I missed my mammaw being right over the hill and how I could walk to her house when I needed life advice or home cookin'. It was time to say goodbye to Tennessee for a while.

I messaged my cousin in Arizona and asked if she had room for visitors. She and her husband owned a dog training business out in the high desert. I figured properly training the dogs would be a good start to our trip across the country. She said we were welcomed for as long as we wanted to stay. I called Dad and told him I was leaving Tennessee, and he knew that I was serious this time.

My dad's younger sister, Amelia, lived in Jacksonville about five hours from my grandparents. She'd checked in with me regularly over the years and had felt like another mother when I was growing up. I'd spent many summers at her house. She invited me out to stay with her until I saved up my first couple checks to head West.

On my last night in Tennessee, I invited over a few close friends for a going-away bonfire. I had donated most of my belongings to a nearby thrift store and given away whatever else to friends. We burned the remainder of leftover stuff in spirit of a new journey to come.

A dear buddy of mine, Chris, took me out for one last Taco Bell run. We sat in the parking lot talking about life. I was scared to leave Tennessee and confided in him that night. He told me to "just go" and said, "Tennessee will always be here." We took a bundle of tacos back to the house and sang the night away. I was sad to leave Gilly and Booker. They were the best roommates I'd ever had.

I had dreamt of going back out West since that time my grandparents took me to Wyoming where I first saw the Tetons. I bought myself a GPS and hit the road first thing that next morning, with a duffle bag of clothes, my bongos, and the dogs.

My mind was set on nothing but the road ahead.

3

The Wait

Summers spent at Aunt Amelia's house were a nice change of scenery. We'd go to the beach, hang by the pool, watch movies, and catch up on life. It was a home away from home. I confided in her and told her dark secrets of mine and my mother's past, things I never knew who else to talk to about. Amelia said it was a good thing that I left Tennessee. She shared stories with me of her times living out West and how California was a must-visit. She talked highly of the Pacific Coast and mentioned that I had to check out Big Sur and Monterey. We talked for hours and watched chick flicks like old times. She introduced me to Jack Kerouac, and I couldn't believe I hadn't read *On the Road* sooner.

Though it was nice to be out of Tennessee, I felt out of place staying at my aunt's house. I wasn't an 11-year-old girl on summer break anymore. I was a 22-year-old *adult* trying to figure life out. I needed to get back on the road. I moped around her house, counting the days until my first check arrived. I was a total bummer to be around for my younger cousins who looked up to me. All I could think about was leaving Mom at that hospital in Alabama and wondering if she was safe.

I took a long walk to the alligator restaurant down the street to clear my head. I ordered a couple beers and realized it was the Fourth of July. I walked back to my aunt's house, locked myself in the guest room, and cried. My uncle tapped on the door and asked if we could talk. He asked what was wrong, but I didn't feel like I could explain it right. I was grieving my mother, and she was still alive. He called my dad and told him I was acting *off*. Then, Dad called and asked if he could accompany me on my road trip to Arizona. He said my aunt agreed to take care of my grandparents for a week, so he and I could spend some time together. I told him I would love that, and he made plans to meet me in Jacksonville.

I felt a burst of energy knowing that we'd be on the road in a few days. I set an alarm for 3:00 a.m. and jarred my two cousins out of bed the following morning. "Come on, we've got to make it in time for sunrise!" I told them. They were excited and jumped right in the car. We did this often during summer visits when they were little

We pulled up to Mickler Beach at dawn and sat by the seashore anticipating the sunrise. Early into the morning, the sky became saturated in melon orange and deep ruby. It was as beautiful as it ever was. I piggybacked my younger cousin across the ocean front, as we laughed and chased her older brother. Water splashed up the back of my legs, as I stretched out my arms and pretended to be a seagull. I traced my toes through the wet sands of the Atlantic Ocean, knowing it may be my last time on this side of the country for a while.

Dad arrived with my grandparents in the next couple days, and we spent the evening talking over dinner. We played a game of Rummikub. Grandma couldn't remember how to play with her Alzheimer's, but Grandpa was still sharp on his board game skills. He won every game. I tickled Grandma in the same spots I always did, and she giggled that wonderful laugh of hers. I talked to her about my plan to travel the West just like she and Grandpa did. She hummed her favorite songs and kept a sweet smile across her rosy cheeks.

The next morning, Dad loaded his bag into the trunk of the Merc. My grandpa hugged me and said, "Send pictures of her out West." He was talking about the car, of course. I hugged the rest of our family, my grandparents, Aunt Amelia, uncle, and cousins, and we were officially hitting the road to go West. We did the "endless wave" until our car was out of sight around the corner. It was an old tradition my grandparents had started many moons ago in their days of traveling. Wave and honk until you can't see each other, until the next time around.

4

"Nothing behind me, everything ahead of me..."

Our hood pointed west. I was happy to be starting the first leg of the journey with my pop. Our first stop was Bourbon Street. Neither of us had been before. We parked the Merc and walked around for an hour with the dogs, bopping into a few shops, and then got right back on the road. An old itch was being scratched, and the air seemed fresher with each mile!

Next, we went to The Alamo and booked a pet-friendly hotel. The dogs barked relentlessly as Dad and I slid out of the hotel to check out downtown San Antonio. It was nice to spend this time with him. I'd missed our time together over the last few years while he'd been taking care of my grandparents in Florida. We walked around downtown observing old architecture and local art. I snapped a few pics with my Nikon camera. We had a late picnic lunch overlooking the Riverwalk and watched a duck family float about downstream. I had a flashback to walking the Riverwalk a decade before on the trip West with my grandparents. I was so grateful to have this time exploring the country with my dad.

We drove farther to Big Bend National Park in Texas and stayed right outside of Terlingua in an off-grid motel with zero cell reception. The sky was a dark blanket with shredded holes of brightly exposed stars and infinite galaxies.

We drove out a few miles from the motel and stopped by the park entrance to observe the night sky. We witnessed the Milky Way in full vibrance, and I was captivated by how bright the stars were out there. We went to lay on the car roof and Dad said, "Hurry, get back in the car!" We both jumped in so quickly our shoes nearly fell off! He pointed from inside the car, doors now locked shut, and said, "There! A mountain lion!" I gasped and squinted forward to two squinty eyes peering back at me. I remember thinking, *How lucky are we, to not be that thing's dinner tonight!* Dad turned on the headlights, and we realized it was simply the reflection of the park sign that read *Big Bend*. We looked at each other and laughed 'til we cried. Still a bit spooked, we observed the stars a little while longer from inside the car.

The next day, we set sails to New Mexico. I had scribbled *White Sands National Monument* onto our trip itinerary. Following the GPS, we ended up on a dead-end road somewhere along military ground. There were several yellow caution signs for *Tank Crossing*, and a military official forced us to turn back around. On the way out, we saw a large bird preying on rattlesnake roadkill. It gave us both the heebie jeebies. A couple hours and detours later, we drove past the San Andreas Mountain Range and arrived at White Sands. The sand sure was white and as powdery as beaches on the Gulf. Dad held the dogs, and I strapped into my snowboard and marked "sandboarding" off my bucket list.

Our final stop of the road trip was my cousin's house in Southern Arizona, after driving roughly 1,900 miles. My cousins were excited to have visitors and welcomed the dogs to sleep in their house. It was nice not worrying about where the dogs were and weren't allowed. My cousin, Beth, and her husband Nicholas seemed to love dogs more than people. Beth showed us around Southern Arizona to some of her favorite spots, and first up was Bisbee. It was an artsy town located 15 minutes from the Mexican Border. The houses surrounding the community were stacked tight like something I'd seen in a travel guide for Italy. It was nice to catch up with family and visit them in their desert environment. We stopped at a brewery for a pint and chatted away the evening.

Around my cousin's house, we observed rattlesnakes, tarantulas, and scorpions right in their backyard. I was cautious everywhere we walked and always felt like some kind of critter was lurking nearby. I took the dogs out for a stroll one morning and got spooked by a dry desert bush blowing in the wind, thinking it was a rattler. I sprinted back to the house and hunched over in the driveway to catch my breath. I was not in Tennessee anymore, and at least my cousin got a kick out of it. As it turned out, it was just a tumbleweed. The mountains in Arizona surprised me at their size, though I was too chicken to hike them solo at the time due to the abundance of poisonous wildlife and mountain lions in the area.

Dad flew back to Florida while I stayed in Arizona. It was bittersweet dropping him off at the airport. I loved having him as a travel companion and also knew I had some soul-searching to do. This was really it. I was miles away from Tennessee and really out there doing it. I wrote in my journal every night and found some comfort in knowing Mom was getting help.

After a few canine training sessions with my cousins, which trained me more than the dogs, I was ready to keep traveling. I wasn't sure where I would go but found great satisfaction in the unknown on the road. I had been flirting with the idea of driving to Cali and knew of a friend staying down in San Diego.

Late one night, as I was journaling in bed, I received a voicemail notification. I didn't have great cell service in Arizona, which I was cool with. It was my mother. After 23 days, she'd been released from the hospital in Alabama and taxied home to Tennessee. I was relieved she'd made it home and equally relieved that I'd skipped town. Gilly and Booker, still living in the house with the one-sided white picket fence, told me that she showed up on the doorstep. They told her I had moved out of state. The thought of her standing there in my absence broke my heart a little more. I felt like I had let her down and knew I needed to take care of myself for a little while. Gilly said she looked better than before and that she cried when they told her I had left. I wasn't quite ready to speak to her, though.

The day before I planned to leave Southern Arizona for Cali, I got a message from a friend back in Tennessee, Barry. He tossed out the idea of flying to Phoenix to check out a university that was well known for organic medicine.

I did a quick Google search and found it was only a three-hour drive north to Phoenix from my cousin's house. "Book it one way!" I told him.

I picked up Barry at Phoenix Sky Harbor International Airport after circling around a few more times than I'd like to admit. The ramps were confusing and a little more intricate than our small country airport back home in the Tri-Cities. It was nice to see a friendly face, and it had been a while since Barry and I hung out. We grabbed some lunch and searched for a hotel. It was 100 degrees there in the concrete jungle, and everything was hot to the touch. We found a room, and Barry paid since I'd made the drive up to fetch him. The presidential debates were scheduled that night, so I settled to stay in with the pups, while Barry ventured out to explore apartments near the college. While getting myself hyped up, because I love a good presidential debate, I found a local Walgreens within walking distance. I scooped up some fun, new hair dye, and put a few blue streaks through my dark brown hair. Barry came back to find that the room smelled thickly of hair bleach.

The next day, I dropped him off to meet with a school advisor and picked him up a couple hours later. He mentioned a girl we went to high school with was chilling down in San Diego, and I said, "Hot dog, let's go to Cali!" We checked out of the hotel en route to check into California! It was a neat thing about road tripping the country. It seemed there were adventures to be had in every direction and especially those pulling us to Cali.

I played Zeppelin's "Going to California" on repeat along with Tupac's "California Love" and, okay, Phantom Planet's "California." We passed a sign that read *Welcome to California*, and I screamed with excitement! I rolled the windows down, took a deep breath, and let the wild in. We were riding by the seats of our pants. Some miles later, we stumbled upon Joshua Tree National Park and found ourselves in unfamiliar territory.

"Isn't this like a famous place to visit?" Barry asked.

"Yeah, I think so," I said.

We followed the dirt road that led us further into Joshua Tree National Park and saw some...Joshua Trees. The car died exactly where we had zero cell reception but with splendid views. I snapped a pic of the Merc for Grandpa, checked the oil, and we walked around for a bit to let her cool down. It was hotter than refried beans outside. We took in the opportunity to witness some cool vegetation in what seemed to be the middle of a desert. After cooling down for a while, the Merc miraculously started back up. We looked at each other and never said a word, making our way back out of Joshua Tree National Park and onward to the Pacific Coast.

On the way to San Diego, we took a detour through Palm Springs to mark "sit on *I Love Lucy* bench" off my bucket list. I had dreamt of seeing that bench statue since I was an elementary school girl. The feeling of seeing it in person, off the internet, was emancipating. It was too hot for the dogs to walk on the sidewalk in Palm Springs, so we made it quick. I snapped a pic with concrete-Lucille for the scrapbook, and we hopped back in the car.

We got back on the road and passed a field full of windmills generating electricity that literally blew our minds. I had never seen anything like them in Tennessee. I pulled over to gawk at the windmills the way some people gawk at highway wrecks. Barry and I drove down some major backroads, jamming and sharing songs with one another. It was a joy to have him as company on the road. As we got closer to wherever it was we were going, we hit major five-lane traffic. Then, we saw green signs leading to San Diego. We were getting pulled by the universe deeply into SoCal and didn't even realize it. Barry called up our friend, Cheyenne. She gave us directions to meet her at some small town right by the ocean. I don't even remember the name of it, but that's where I had my first-ever California Burrito. Steak, fresh avocado, and French fries rolled snugly in a grand tortilla. My life had changed forever.

Upon Cheyenne joining our brigade, we looked for a place to camp for the night. We checked out the spot by the beach where we had eaten burritos, but the lot was at max capacity for overnighters. Cheyenne was the most free-spirited person I'd ever met. She was always down for the ride without knowing where we were going. A friend of hers recommended a camping spot at Black's Beach, so we followed the coordinates farther south. We pulled onto a college campus and followed signs for free weekend parking. The signs led us up a five-story car garage where we parked the Merc for the night. I snapped another pic for Grandpa and loaded up my backpack with a tent, sleeping bag, and food for the pups. I felt like I'd come prepared. I leashed up the dogs and followed Cheyenne and Barry down a flight of stairs to the sidewalk. "I think it's this way," Cheyenne said. Barry and I shrugged and put our full faith in her directions under the moonlit sky. Everything was closed and mostly dark around the town, except for the occasional headlights of weekend college kids out on the prowl.

We followed Cheyenne to a large dirt wall with a huge stone staircase that went on for as far as we could see into the night. We trailed down step after step for what seemed half an hour until our feet touched sand. We had made it to the Pacific Ocean. I threw my bag down, dropped the dog's leashes, and sprinted to the seaside. I dipped my toes into the Pacific Ocean for the first time in my life and thanked Cheyenne for this wonderful plan. The stars were holy-bright and seemed to emancipate the sky. The air was as crisp as I'd dreamt any mysterious summer night on the West Coast would be.

We pitched our tents and saw a roaring fire farther down the beach. We followed our hearts into the night and met a friendly group of college kids, most around our age or within a year or two. I was tired from the day's drive and turned in early with the dogs, excited to sleep in my tent nestled along the Pacific Coastline. Barry and Cheyenne stayed up around the campfire, catching up from lost time. I lay there in my tent, appreciating every second of all of it. I had used that same tent to camp back home in the Appalachian Mountains. I had set it up and camped on Roan Mountain and at Laurel Falls more times than I could count, and now here it sat perched by the Pacific Ocean underneath the California starlit sky. It was a magical first night in the Golden State.

The next morning, I woke up and stepped outside the tent feeling like I was in a dream. The ocean stretched for miles along huge rocky cliffs. Barry and Cheyenne woke up not long after, and we were all on the same page about craving breakfast. While packing up the tent, I noticed something uncanny off in the distance. Why, it was a naked old man! No underwear, swimsuit, or shirt. He was bare-chested and ballsy—literally!

"Oh, I forgot to mention that this is a nude beach!" Cheyenne said. *Wow, okay*, I thought, *something unplanned for the bucket list*. I had never been to a nude beach before, and what a surprise it was! Cheyenne and I threw our shirts and bras off and raced to the ocean water, with our hair blowing wildly in the wind. The dogs chased behind, running back and forth through the sand. I leapt giddily, jumping wave after wave. My lips were wet with saltwater and tasted like pure freedom! Barry sat back by the camp with an ear-to-ear grin just taking it all in. I laughed until my cheeks hurt and for the first time in a while felt like I could breathe again.

We climbed up the long staircase that ascended the hidden nude beach. I offered to retrieve the car if my friends agreed to keep an eye on the dogs. On the walk up the hill leading to the parking garage, I thought about what an amazing trip this had been already. I felt totally free out in the world, walking up some random sidewalk in SoCal with my tent in my backpack, carrying everything I needed. I had awoken from a great night's sleep on sands by the Pacific Ocean with no plans and no major commitments for the days to come. Cheyenne had been a godsend on this journey and was awakening my soul to new depths. I found the car and drove over to pick up the gang with the stereo blasting some California techno-vibes.

Mako, my former Colorado-adventure snowboarding comrade, sent a text reminding me he was chilling down in San Diego. He invited me to come out and stay with him in Imperial Beach, as he was down there house-sitting for a friend. I called to let him know I was headed south from Black's Beach and had two extra passengers. He kindly called up his buddy and got the okay for us all to come couch surf for a few days. We set the GPS to Imperial Beach and pulled up to a quaint white house with a small fenced-in yard, perfect for the dogs to have space to roam. I hugged Mako and thanked him for having us. It was good to see him again, a dear friend who was so welcoming and shared a passion for travel. And the world was our oyster!

Mako broke out the guitar that night along with a hand drum that hung on the wall for decoration. Without much anticipation, we all started jamming together. Barry and Mako took turns with the instruments, and Cheyenne and

I sang along in rhythm. I called Dad to let him know I was still alive, *very much alive*. I told him about camping out at Black's Beach and how it had turned out to be a nude beach. After a long pause in the conversation, he busted out laughing. Then, he confessed that he and a college friend had taken a road trip to California back in the day. He said that they had also ended up camping on Black's Beach, totally unplanned, and learned of it being a nude beach! I couldn't believe it. It was some stars-aligning, universe-speaking soul stuff, and California was filled with magic in the air. After a wholesome jam session with Mako, we all slept soundly for a night of much needed rest.

Mako grew very fond of both Cheyenne and Barry and took us all on a personal tour of the Navy base, where he'd spent some time working, and around downtown San Diego. We had lunch at a local food truck, and it seemed only natural to order another California Burrito. Towering buildings lured us in after sunset for a few drinks within the downtown cityscape. Barry and Cheyenne wandered off to go dancing, and Mako and I caught up on life.

"A lot has happened since Vail," I told him.

"So, what's next, Millie," he asked, "after San Diego?"

I pondered the question. "I don't really know. I have been thinking about Driggs," I said.

"What's there for you? Isn't that no man's land?" he asked.

"The Tetons and big winters. I want to end up somewhere with a lot of snow," I said.

"I have never heard of Driggs until you. Why would you go somewhere that I've never even heard of?" he asked.

"That's what makes it such a special place, Mako. And besides, I want to go somewhere where I can make my own decisions. Away from it all. Somewhere where life is on my terms, you know?" I said.

"You are crazy, Millie. That is what I know," he said.

We laughed and finished our drinks, then took off to find the rest of the crew. And then, we danced the night away. The next day, we slept in through early afternoon and woke up with a fierce appetite. Without any disagreement, we all decided on a Chinese buffet for lunch.

"What does your fortune cookie say?" I asked Cheyenne.

"In your 20s, a mystery. Your 30s, pull together. And 40s, reach back to see how far you've come," she said.

My mouth fell open. "I got the exact same fortune!"

Barry grinned and said, "I got the same one, too!"

We all looked at Mako, as he stuffed his mouth with Chinese doughnuts.

"Well, what does it say?" I asked.

He took off the plastic wrapper and read aloud, "A good lunch makes a good man."

We belted out laughing as Mako finished his dessert. We spent the evening on the beach. Though we were together, it seemed we each enjoyed our own silent bliss. That was California. There was not a care in the world, and everyone was always outside in the open air, and smiling. People were always outside, al fresco, everywhere we went, flying kites or hanging out in groups of loved ones. San Diego was filled with life!

I was relieved the dogs could stay in the house while we explored San Diego to avoid the coastal heat. However, after a day out exploring, we came back to a shredded surprise. I walked in the front door, and Mako's face flushed red.

"Millie! I did not tell them we had dogs staying here! You said they were trained," he said.

Luna had chewed through a size 11 leather boot that belonged to Mako's dear friend, who was so kindly letting us all stay in his home free of charge while he was away serving our country on military business.

"Oh no, I'll figure this out," I said.

I searched the internet for the same style and size of leather boots. It would take them several weeks to arrive if I ordered them brand new, totaling $300 plus shipping. I glanced a side-eye at Luna and asked, "You couldn't have chewed the dollar-store house slippers instead, right beside the leather boots?" She had good taste.

Mako and I each popped open a Filipino beer from the local grocer and hung in for the night. I hunted around on eBay and found the same size shoe with a winning bid for $180. It was not in the budget, but I felt a load of relief and sent Mako's friend a personal message with a most sincere apology. He was content, and I was thankful he continued to let us stay in his house for the rest of the week.

When Cheyenne and Barry returned, we all took a walk down to the ocean-front. I remember skipping alongside Cheyenne and us both giddy with laughter. We ran up to a group on the beach and joined a spur of the moment sand volleyball game with Mako and Barry. There were no feelings of competitiveness, and usually I was very competitive when it came to sports. Cheyenne and I took off our shoes and walked barefoot side by side through the sand closer to the water. "You look so happy," she said to me, mirroring my energy. In that moment, I remember what it felt like for the very first time to feel *blissed out*. That's the only way I can describe it. Watching those Pacific waves crash joyfully. Feeling the California sunshine effortlessly transpire into an inspiring sunset. Cruising through this state, windows down, listening to "Coming Home" by Leon Bridges. That's what it all felt like at that very moment. I took a deep breath and sat down right beside her, sharing smiles, then the guys sat down beside us. It was a picture-perfect moment, us four in the prime days of our youth, blissfully unaware and needing to be nowhere.

The next day, Cheyenne and Barry stayed in to work on writing and editing photos. I went with Mako to have dinner with a former military friend of his, Z. They had been friends since meeting long ago in the Navy. There was also JJ, who was an amazing basketball player. I met Z's whole family and became great friends with his daughters. They convinced me to try squid for the first time, another new one for the bucket list. We played a couple rounds of 23 in their backyard on the cement ball court. Z and JJ grilled up some amazing new foods for lunch, traditional Filipino dishes. And we ended the night with family-style karaoke, singing Journey's "Don't Stop Believing" with hugs all around.

Our time together in San Diego was coming to an end. Cheyenne made plans to ride with friends to Las Vegas, and Mako was preparing for the drive home to San Francisco. I wasn't sure of my plans yet, but I had been spending a lot of time applying for seasonal jobs around Driggs, Idaho. I had a phone interview with the ticket sales department at Grand Targhee Resort our last night in San Diego. I was offered the job contingent upon finding housing for the winter months. I reached out to a few people in the area and contacted a guy named Luke on Craigslist about a room rental he had recently listed. It seemed like roommates were necessary to afford the cost of living out there. He messaged me back to "keep in touch" and let him know when I got to the valley for a tour of the room.

I aimed to be in Idaho by September to allow a few weeks to bop around Cali some more and keep road trippin'. Plus, this would give me time to secure lodging before the big snow season. Mako invited me up to San Francisco. It was about an eight-hour drive from where we were. He had to get back home to start his college classes, so I told him I'd meet him up there. *Why not?* I wanted to take the scenic route up Highway 1 to Big Sur, like Aunt Amelia had suggested. Barry decided to ride to Vegas with Cheyenne and see where it led him. We spent our final night together with one more jam sesh, pulling the drum off the wall and into our circle. Mako and I wrote a song together that night that would stick in my head for the rest of the summer.

"San Diego":

I want to wake up, feel free, and let go
What better place than down in San Diego
Where folks vibe happy, Pacific waves crash
Everyone stays active 'stead of sittin' on their ass
Take me some place where I can live
Somewhere with opportunity, so I can give
My all to this world I love

We packed up our things the next morning. It was bittersweet, as the journey was parting us in different ways. We had shared such a magical time in San Diego. I hugged Cheyenne tightly, and my eyes watered. Barry helped throw my bags in the trunk of the Merc and thanked me for driving him out there. We said our goodbyes, more like "see ya laters." Or as me and my dad tell each other, *See ya when I see ya.* Barry and Cheyenne rode off down the road with a friend who scooped them up in a van. I watched them and waved until they were out of sight. Mako started his car after giving me directions to follow him north for a few hours. He said there was a special exit to take to get to Highway 1 and that we'd stop for gas, so he could point me in the right direction. Eyes still watering into a light, happy cry, the dogs and I took off waving goodbye to the magic of SoCal and on to the next.

5

Going Anywhere

I jammed the radio, windows down, and followed Mako up the interstate. *What a life*, I thought. Avocado trees flew by in a blur alongside the road. Cars zoomed by, weaving in and out of lanes. I felt so inspired along the drive that I turned off the radio and began singing lyrics to my own song.

People, always gotta go somewhere
And people, are always on a schedule
But time's not tangible
Me, I'm just going anywhere
Taking roads that lead nowhere
Letting time just disappear

People, always gotta be something
And people, always need a special ring
A way to prove their being
Why don't you just come along with me
We could show the world a different theme
Show them all how to be free

Mako pulled off the exit and up to a gas station to refuel. He told me this is where we would split ways. I thanked him for everything and half-smiled as we parted ways. The dogs and I were now off the highway, *off the beaten path*, and following the flow of a mysterious winding road. After miles of bare ground, the landscape changed into beautiful hues of greens and browns. It was prime Californian wine country! I was gleefully caught off guard by miles of rolling vineyards. I'd never seen anything like it. Majestic, tangled grapevines were in every direction, entwined fearlessly around rustic fencing for as far as the eye could see. I followed the curvy roads for hours until it dumped us along Pacific Coast Highway 1.

I felt rebirthed at the sight of the California coastline. Chills ran down my arms, and I was overwhelmingly filled with peace. Wild seals hung out on big chunks of rock casually as clouds in the sky. The road curved up and around large cliffs that dropped what seemed leagues to the sea below. Waves crashed upward toward the road as if to boast, *Welcome, welcome to the ends of the earth!* The warm but not hot breeze blew my hair out the window, and the sunshine softly kissed my arm. I tapped my fingers along the door to my own music. This was California. Every mile brought a freeing sense of place within this great, big world. *I belong!* I wondered if I could just stay in this moment forever.

Before I could count all the seals, I was driving over Bixby Bridge where Jack Kerouac himself used to sit below the beams, writing his own beautiful words. I pulled over to take in the moment and capture a few precious photos with the Nikon. I had dreamt of traveling to this exact spot and could hardly believe I'd made it. I said a silent thank you to Aunt Amelia, and the universe, for instilling a connection with this place. I swallowed up the Pacific breeze and the thoughts of Jack pacing around the same terrace that the dogs and I sat on. I snapped a quick pic for Grandpa. After taking it all in, I nodded *see ya later* to ole Bixby and jumped back into the Merc. The dogs were excited, feeding off my energy and the random belts of squealing I let out along the drive. I was so excited I could hardly contain myself. We were moments away from Big Sur, and I could feel it with every bone in my body.

After a few more jaw-dropping turns, we were officially welcomed to Big Sur by a quaint wooden sign. I grounded myself and decided to press onward to Mako's where I knew a bed was waiting. It had been a long day of driving, and I didn't want to rush my time in Big Sur. We were three hours from Vallejo where Mako lived, just outside of San Fran. He'd agreed to come back to Big Sur with me and be my tour guide after some rest.

The dogs and I cruised through Monterey Bay and stopped for dinner at the beloved 24-hour Jack in the Box. I had found a new sweet spot for the grease of a Buttery Jack burger with jalapeños. I hopped on the interstate to San Francisco and met Mako at a nearby gas station. We were always having run-ins at fuel stops, it seemed. His family lived in a beautiful house out in the suburbs of Vallejo. They welcomed me with open arms, and his aunt made us beef pasties for dinner. They were so good, stuffed with spicy pork covered in gravy, and the bread was so warm and sweet. I couldn't recall the last time I'd eaten a home-cooked meal.

Mako had school the next day, so I hung out and recorded our "San Diego" song in his spare bedroom/studio. After school, he took me to explore wine country up in Napa Valley. We drove around to a couple of his favorite vineyards and snuck a few fresh grapes right from the vines. We bought some cheese and a bit of wine to sip later that evening, as we recorded some music together. I felt so welcomed into his family's home and loved trying all the new Filipino comfort foods.

Later that night, I surrendered to a slew of missed calls from my mom. It was the first I'd spoken with her since the incident in Alabama. I told her I was traveling the West Coast. She was stable enough to make full sentences and hold a rational conversation throughout the entire call. I wasn't sure how I felt. It gave me a lot of hope that her mind could heal. She asked when I was coming home, and I told her I just wanted to keep exploring for a while.

Mako only went to school two days a week, so we had plenty of time to hang out. He drove us out to the city by the bay. I cried at my first sighting of the Golden Gate Bridge. It was beautiful. All I could hear in my delusional state of happiness were the song lyrics by Scott McKenzie, "If you're going to

San Francisco," which I did, naturally, have flowers in my hair. That was another check off the bucket list. I was pouring over with bliss, high on California
vibes. We went to a university art museum with beautiful outdoor sculptures,
ate egg rolls in Chinatown, and visited the antique penny arcade. We checked
out the seals at Fisherman's Wharf, which were totally Moe's spirit animals. I
had fallen for San Diego, and now San Fran was whisking me away.

Later that night as I was journaling, an idea blossomed. I wanted to find a
way to keep traveling. This was real living, and I wanted to make a lifestyle out
of it. I thought of ways to eliminate steep food costs by learning how to hunt
and to grow a garden full of colorful vegetables. I dreamt of raising chickens
that laid eggs. Rent had been my biggest expense back home, before I had left
it all behind to travel the country. I yearned to figure out a way to live more
sustainably and without big overhead costs going to a landlord and utilities
each month. I thought for a few moments, and it dawned on me. I could save
up money and buy a shed (a shell for a tiny house). I sketched it out in my journal. I needed to save $4,000. Then, I'd insulate it and renovate the interior to
convert it into a livable dwelling. I vented the idea to Mako over breakfast the
next morning. He said, "Millie, you're crazy," and insisted that I wouldn't follow through with it. I half agreed with him.

I turned a page in the journal and let those thoughts idle. "Are you ready to
go see Big Sur today?" Mako asked. I choked and could only reply with an eager
nod. We left the dogs at Mako's house and ventured back out to the magical
coastline. It was a day I'd never want to end, the kind that seems to fly away in
a blur. First, we climbed up the large ocean rocks at Pfeiffer Beach. We sat up
there for an hour whale watching. It tempted my wildest dreams to come true
at the bare thought of seeing a whale swim across the panoramic ocean view in
front of us. Big Sur was a fairytale, and I pretended to be a woodland fairy elf
queen for the day, exploring uncharted lands and blazing new trails. I didn't
want to climb down off that rock. I thought I'd set up my tent and just live up
there until I saw a whale or the waves washed me away—whichever came first.

With no whales in sight, it was on to the next adventure. We sailed the
Merc vessel onward and parallel parked behind a row of cars. I followed Mako

down a winding path leading us closer towards the ocean. I parted through a crowd to witness a beautiful flowing waterfall pouring off the cliff down into turquoise waters below, meeting the ocean with such grace.

"We have to go down there so I can dip my toes in that water," I told Mako.

"No way, you'll get in trouble," he said.

I attempted to climb down closer to the falls and away from the crowd, but Mako convinced me it was a bad idea for the sake of keeping the place mysterious and preserved. I'd been used to having less crowded waterfalls back in Appalachia, often all to myself to swim and frolic as I pleased. I agreed with Mako and observed the waterfall's beauty from a distance, though my soul yearned to submerge my entire body into those glittering turquoise waters. We walked back up the path and found an intersection that led to another trail. We hiked along it for a couple miles, and it opened up to pristine views of huge rock faces and ocean stretching for miles on end. For a moment, it felt like we were living in prehistoric times and that a Pterodactyl may swoop by any minute. Big Sur had forever captured my heart. I felt alive and well, becoming one with the Wild West.

Back in Vallejo, I was itching to get back on the pavement, between those yellow lines. I craved the inspiration that flowed when the road met the sky and for miles, I just drove. Big Sur added fuel to the fire, and I knew there were uncharted lands out there calling to be explored. I told Mako I was leaving the next morning for Driggs, Idaho. It was about 12 hours away.

I texted Luke, the guy from Craigslist, and told him I'd be in Driggs soon if he wanted to talk more about rental arrangements. We agreed to keep in touch over Facebook until I made it out to Idaho. Mako insisted I check out Tahoe. He said I would love it, plus it was only slightly out of the way. He said if I waited until the weekend, he'd come and show me around and we could stay for free at a casino in Reno. But the road was calling. I thanked him for showing me graciously around California and hugged him tight, not knowing when we'd see each other again. The dogs and I hit the asphalt sea, and it was official. We were en route to Teton Valley.

Two hours into the drive, I couldn't ignore the signs for South Lake Tahoe.

At the last one, I said, "Ah, what the heck" and followed the road off the exit. I guess we were going to Tahoe after all. The curvy pass led down into a town boasting giant pine trees and steep, rocky mountain views. Everything smelled of wilderness and rustic heaven. I had no idea Tahoe was so wild and dense with the glory of infinite hiking trails in what seemed all directions, all at once. California was a trip; from the sea to the mountains, we'd go!

6

The Cards We're Dealt

I arrived at South Lake, seemingly pulled in by the universe herself. I didn't know the difference between the North and South Lakes; South just sounded *familiar*. I stopped at a gas station to fill up and got distracted by the souvenir stand. I bought my first souvenir of the trip, aside from all the rocks I'd been collecting. There was a navy-blue Lake Tahoe hoodie that called my name and turned out to be my favorite article of clothing for the rest of the trip. The dogs and I had only scratched the surface of this place, literally just pulling in to fill up the gas tank, and I already loved it. Mako was right.

As we got closer to the lake, the trees continued to thicken and get taller. Everything smelled of pine! The Auto Zone is what officially sold me on Lake Tahoe. It wasn't your ordinary white, orange, and red auto shop. It was made to look like a rustic wooden cabin and soon, I realized the whole town was rustically designed to accentuate wilderness. I wasn't sure where we'd sleep that night, and I'd saved up an extra check to get to Idaho comfortably. I decided to use part of it on a motel to get some rest and a feel for our bearings. This place was totally worth exploring more. The off-season rates were surprisingly affordable for being near the base of Heavenly Ski Resort.

The dogs and I checked in and got our motel key. Then, I unlocked the door and realized why it was so cheap. The bed hugged all four corners of the wall, and the bathroom was just enough room to squat. I was totally cool with it, because we were in Tahoe, man! I took a shower and Googled hikes around the area. I learned of the Tahoe Rim Trail and put it on the future bucket list, because it required an advance reservation. I sat on the motel bed wondering where to begin in this wilderness wonderland.

There was a local brewery nearby, and that seemed a good place to start. I ordered a nice summer citrus beer. Dan was a friendly local who immediately started up a conversation after I placed my order in what he called a "sweet Southern accent." We split an order of nachos and talked about our favorite baseball teams and mountain towns of the West. He was a Giants fan, and I was a lifelong Cardinals fan being that my dad was from St. Louis.

While sipping my beer, I got a text from Mako that read, "I can't believe you left when your team is in town." My eyes honed in on the screenshot he sent next. The Cardinals were playing the Giants that week. *A big bucket list item for me.* I spoke with Dan about this dilemma and mentioned I'd just left San Fran earlier that morning. "Well, they aren't playing until Friday, and you could always drive back," he said. And, he had a great point. I was on zero time restrictions. Dan talked about a few good hikes around the area and suggested we go on one the following day after he got off work.

I woke up and checked out of the motel with the pups. We drove around exploring different roads that followed the lake. Tahoe was amazing, and everything was centered around nature. I came across a dog-friendly beach and parked for the afternoon to take a swim. Luna did victory rolls in the sand, and Moe chased rocks in the lake. I basked in the California sun thinking I may never leave.

A friendly stranger approached us with her three dogs and sat a chair down beside our blanket. "Hello, I'm Val," she said. I introduced myself and the dogs. We talked for the next few hours as though we were long lost friends. She told me of her children and grandchildren. And I told her of my trip across the country. I hadn't stopped to think of it as that before. I had driven across the country from the East Coast to the West Coast, the Atlantic Ocean to the Pacific. It had turned into quite a journey, and I was thankful to have met Val to reflect upon it with.

It was a beautiful day on the lake, and I didn't feel a care in the world. I followed the dogs into the crisp, clear water and took a refreshing dip. Tahoe had some of the prettiest rocks I'd ever seen, and I gathered some up for our collection. The air around the lake was clean and healing. I took turns between swimming and drying in the sun while sharing the day with Val and her pup gang. I asked for her phone number so we could keep in touch.

I loaded up the dogs, and we drove over to the wooden grocery store to meet Dan. We went in to buy some Lagunitas and hot dogs after deciding to camp out that night. Dan suggested a spot he knew with a view. I offered to drive since he had become my Tahoe guide. Going down the main strip, a medium-sized black bear casually walked across both lanes of traffic right in front of us. "Happens all the time," he said. We cut a hard left and drove up a steep hill that climbed up the mountain. He said, "Park it right here." I looked at him, confused. We were right in front of someone's vacation home. He assured me that he camped along this trail quite often with friends, so I went with my gut on it. I was ready for more hiking and camping. *Always ready.*

We followed the trail up three miles to incredible views of the lake. I unpacked the tent and set it up while Dan set up his. "Wait until you see the stars out here," he said. I couldn't wait. The dogs roamed nearby exploring all the new scents. Dan built a fire, and we each had a brew and got to know each other a little better. He made fun of my Tennessean accent, and I laughed at everything out of pure giddiness. Then, as it got darker, something rustled in the trees and spooked me. "There are mountain lions all over these woods," Dan said. I casually gulped and scanned my surroundings. Then, out from behind a tree, Moe ran up and licked my cheek. I was relieved and stayed on high alert pretty much all night, thinking of possible lurking mountain lions.

Dan and I chatted about life and our different upbringings. He had skied since he was an infant and grew up in mountain town culture, and my roots were thick in the Appalachian Mountains of the South. I had learned to snowboard on pure ice and sometimes even mud. As the night went on with more mysterious sounds in the woods, I jumped into my tent with the dogs. I asked Dan to bring his sleeping bag over to our tent to protect us from the mountain lions, and he didn't resist. We stayed up late talking, eventually laughing ourselves to sleep. Moe slept inside my sleeping bag right at my feet, and Luna along my side.

I awoke to a tug on my hair, and Dan said, "Quick, come out here!" I stepped outside the tent into the early dark morning. The sky was perfectly black, with just the right amount of chill in the air to really make the stars pop. I smiled and gave Dan a big hug. Witnessing the Tahoe night sky was invigorating. The stars were so bright, and I felt right where I belonged.

We packed up our gear at sunrise, and I dropped Dan off at work with plans to meet up later and go see a concert by the lake. The dogs and I went exploring some more. We drove uphill around the opposite side of the lake. I parked along the road by a dirt trail and leashed the dogs up for a new hike. The trail went straight up, causing a burning sensation in my thighs. It felt so good to be out exploring! We hiked a couple miles up to a thick wooded area in the forest and climbed over some pretty big boulders. Between the tall, crowded pines, I caught a glimpse of turquoise waters glistening in the sun below us. We kept trekking. Luna hopped up and down from rock to rock, and Moe trailed behind. We reached a small clearing on top of the mountain. There was a stunning alpine lake tucked away in the distance, as blue as a depressed beatnik (referencing Jack Kerouac for those unbeknown). I sat on a large rock with the dogs and took it all in over a peanut butter and banana sandwich. *An Appalachian fave passed down from my mammaw.*

We descended the trail and headed back to our new favorite dog beach for a swim. On the drive down, I got super hungry. On the road, you never knew where or what you'd end up having for lunch. Often, peanut butter sammies from the trunk. We ended up at Taco Bell that evening. I got the power lunch bowl which included rice, beans, tomatoes, and fresh avocado because *California.* It was delicious, some of the freshest avocado I'd ever tasted. As I sat there in the parking lot of T-Bell, "All Apologies" by Nirvana came on the radio. I was having a moment. *I'm exactly where I'm supposed to be.* So, I decided to go get a tattoo!

I met up with Dan, and he took me to his friend's tattoo parlor. I decided to get one on each wrist. *All in All is All We Are* on my right wrist to remind me that we're all one and the same, and all life is interconnected. And on the left, I got the Three Pillars of the Jedi symbols: *The Force, Knowledge,* and *Self-Discipline.* I had read a book from a thrift store back in Arizona about Master Yoda's spiritual teachings and decided this would make a good reminder along the journey of life. You may find The Force, but Self-Discipline takes constant practice. Knowledge is earned, always with room to learn and grow.

The tattoo artist laughed and said, "So you're just a country girl from Tennessee who came all the way to Tahoe to get a Nirvana and *Star Wars* tattoo on the same day?"

I smiled and said, "Yeah, I guess so."

We drove over to the lake after my tattoos were finished. The music was starting soon. All I could think about was that The Cards were playing on the San Francisco Bay the next day. I sent Mako a text and told him to buy two tickets. I hugged Dan and told him I had to get back to the city by the bay to see my fave baseball team play. We enjoyed the sunset by the lake. He laughed and said to come back and visit. The dogs could sense my excitement and seemed to know we were getting back on the road.

7

Subways

I pulled back into Mako's neighborhood, stoked about seeing The Cards play. He showed me the tickets and asked if I was excited. "Are you kidding me?" I asked. "I'm not going to sleep!" We jammed on the piano and guitars for a bit and turned in for the night.

The next day, Mako drove us to his grandpa's house right outside the city to park his car. We walked a couple blocks over to the subway station and got tickets to AT&T Park. I couldn't stop smiling on the subway. It was my first time riding one, and it was a blast! San Fran locals sat casually in corners with their earbuds in or lost in the pages of a book, and here I was standing up with the biggest smile on my face.

We got off the subway and walked several blocks toward the stadium. I was sporting my deepest red, long-sleeve 2011 St. Louis Cardinals World Series shirt in a sea of Giants fans. I was pumped to see Matheny and his gang of birds. We waltzed up into the stadium that hung over the San Francisco Bay. We stood behind the team as they warmed up, and I geeked out pointing at them all in disbelief. "That's really them," I said. Then we went to order my first stadium hot dog, which I was equally as excited for. I dumped on the kraut and mustard and smiled all the way back to our seats. It was Christmas time in my heart, and what a great day for baseball! The Giants made a comeback in the last inning and took it home, but it didn't kill my baseball buzz. I was as giddy as the first inning and just happy to be there, win or lose, cheering on my team.

We exited the stadium, and the streets were flooded with black and orange. Everyone was migrating to the nearest pub. We stopped to have a postgame brew, then continued back for another subway ride. We picked up Mako's car and went back to his family's house, greeted by some very happy pups.

Mako said, "So, does this mean we're heading back to Tahoe tomorrow since it's the weekend?"

And I thought about it for a moment. I was so excited to see the Tetons again for the first time since I was in grade school, and those mountains around Tahoe called to be explored.

"Yeah, sure," I said, "but only for one night."

I followed Mako that morning on the drive back to Tahoe. We took a new route and parked off the road by a sign for a hike. We trekked up four miles with the pups, and Mako became short-winded and said we should turn around. I urged him to keep going as the dogs ran freely ahead of us. We chatted about universities in California and their tuition reimbursement programs. I toyed with the idea of becoming a California resident. We huffed and puffed, and I enjoyed the nice elevation gain. We finally reached the top of the summit, and it was spectacular. There was a picture-perfect opening between two large rock walls that showcased a magnificent view of the lake down below. "I can't believe I've never been here," Mako said. Luna did her victory roll, and Moe skipped back and forth. I glanced through the rocks and took a deep breath. *Wow.*

We followed the trail back to our cars and resumed our course to Reno, Nevada, directly on the border of Tahoe. Mako's family went to a casino there often and had built up enough points for a free stay in a pet-friendly hotel room. We checked in and brought the pups up the elevator. Luna took off running down the hall. Moe looked up at me and casually licked his lips to let me know it was dinner time. Mako swiped the hotel key, and both dogs ran in and jumped on the bed. Mako and I headed down to the main floor to grab dinner. He gambled for a little while, and I quietly observed. I wasn't a gambler myself and watched him play Roulette. I felt lucky, decided to place one bet, and lost $50.

Mako asked me, "What's so special about these Tetons?"

"The Tetons are unexplainable. When I was a kid, my grandparents drove us out there to meet up with my uncle. My dad flew in, and we ended up camping near some hot springs in my uncle's Volkswagen van. It's never left my memory, the feeling I had out there. It's like time just stopped, and we took each moment, day by day under the stars," I said.

It was time for me to get there. I packed my duffle bag that morning and went with Mako to have breakfast at Jack in the Box, because that had become our tradition. We talked about future travels over the pancake platter. I told him he'd better come visit me when I got to wherever it was I was going. I put in the coordinates for Driggs, Idaho, and the dogs and I were officially en route to The Grand Tetons!

8

Back West

We drove through Rexburg, Idaho, also known as "Sexy Rexy" by the locals. We were minutes away from seeing my favorite mountain range in the country. I held my breath and let out a final sigh as The Grand came into view. There she was—the same sharp curves and rock faces that stole my heart in the sixth grade. It felt like I was reuniting with an old friend. I pulled over and snapped a pic of the Merc with the Tetons in the background, for my grandpa. I drove through Driggs and into Victor to visit my uncle, aunt, and cousins. It was my dad's youngest brother and his family. They had offered a place for the dogs and me to stay in their canned ham camper in the side yard.

The canned ham was cozy. It was early fall, which meant vibrant yellow leaves and the possibility of snow at any time up in those higher elevations. I'd made it back in time for a true powder winter and just needed to find housing and officially accept the job at the local ski resort.

I messaged Luke and let him know I had made it to Teton Valley. He said he was busy working over the next few days and that he'd get back to me. In the meantime, I would read a few good books in the canned ham camper, explore local trails, and visit with my family. It was so chilly at night, and I couldn't have been any cozier than I was in my sleeping bag with two snuggling pups. I soaked up views of The Grand right out the window in the evenings from my uncle's backyard.

My dear friend, Chris, from back in Tennessee, messaged me asking how the trip was going. I hadn't talked to him or anyone from back home much since departing Tennessee. He had started working for Delta after I left town and had some miles saved up for a free flight. He mentioned always wanting to visit the Tetons, so I said, "Well, come on out!" He booked a roundtrip flight, and I picked him up a few days later at the Jackson Hole Airport. He was so excited to see the Tetons in person, and who could blame him? When he first arrived, he did multiple handstands out in the field in front of the airport. Chris and I shared a genuine stoke for big mountains and Western culture.

We went to Jackson Hole first, and I took his picture under the antler arches. *Classic.* We explored around Colter Bay and through Grand Teton National Park. Over the next couple days, my aunt invited us to Granite Hot Springs. We met up with her and the rest of the fam and thought we may stay to camp after they left. My uncle led us on a hike to the natural hot springs, where a waterfall flowed above. Moe and I soaked in the springs with my aunt, while Luna chased my cousins around the waterfall. Nothing beats sitting out in the wilderness in a natural hot spring surrounded by tall pines. Truly, this is the environment where I most feel a great sense of belonging and safety within myself.

As nightfall was nearing, my family headed out. Chris and I built up a fire and talked about how grand the Tetons truly were. We talked about how mysterious life felt when you were out in the middle of the woods. We agreed how small we felt out in the world and wanted to explore the West more. Both mindful of the presence of grizzly bears, we decided to move the conversation to the tent with the dogs. Chris slept with Moe, or rather Moe forced his way into Chris's sleeping bag. Naturally, Luna curled up by my side under a small wool blanket. We both kept bear spray right by our sides and dozed off to sounds of a nearby creek.

The next morning, we brewed coffee over the fire and made plans to go explore some sand dunes near Rexburg. I drove us a couple hours from the hot springs to the sand dunes and whipped my snowboard out of the trunk, which had been getting more time in the sand than snow. The dogs followed me up the steep dunes as Chris waved from below. A side-by-side came roaring over the top of the dune and nearly blew my hat off. I strapped in and coasted down the sand at a swift turtle pace, due to the layer of wax that remained from last season. It was steep enough to get a fun ride and fast enough where the dogs kept up behind. Once again, I felt totally in the right place at the right time and was stoked to have a friend to explore the mountains and valleys of Idaho with.

After a couple days of hiking, we retreated back to life in the canned ham camper. Chris slept in the small bed across from me, and we watched *180 Degrees South* his last night in town. It was very fitting to listen to the film's soundtrack. "Here's to Now" by Ugly Casanova was one of my most favorite travel jams. We talked about our dreams and places we wanted to see in the world. I told Chris about my shed/tiny home idea and thoughts of going back to Tennessee for a while if lodging out West didn't pan out. He offered to teach me how to hunt if I did. We were both too stoked to sleep as we listened to the rest of the soundtrack and dreamed of our wildest adventures.

I took him to the airport in the morning. Goodbyes were bittersweet, but they were a given when spending time with friends who'd traveled together. We were always saying goodbyes and see ya laters, nos vamos. I waved to him until he was out of sight and met the dogs back at the Merc.

It got downright chilly over the next few nights, so I spent a lot of time reading and reflecting on my trip thus far in the canned ham. I watched a season of *Mountain Men* on my laptop, a show about living off-grid that Chris had introduced me to. It really made me want to live off the land. I longed for his companionship when I looked at his empty bed across from mine. We'd had such grand adventures in a short time span.

Luke texted me, apologizing, and said his landlord would not allow pets in the rental. I told him not to worry about it, and we remained friends on Facebook. I investigated other options for roommates around the valley. I checked the Facebook community groups, Craigslist, and asked around town. I was not having any luck finding a place that was both affordable and pet-friendly near the ski resort. I was determined to spend the winter in Teton Valley.

The following weekend, I called my mom. I just needed to hear her voice and make sure she was safe. She sounded much better, and it was nice to confide in her. She was coherent and made full sentences still. I mentioned the shed idea to her and that I was thinking about coming home. She said she'd ask my pappaw if I could put a shed on a plot of his land until I saved up for my own acre. I thought it sounded enticing if he was okay with it since winter was nearing, and housing in the Tetons wasn't aligning. My budget was dwindling, and without housing, I couldn't commit to working at the ski resort.

I could go back to Tennessee, get a shed, save up for an acre, and learn to hunt. I tossed around the idea of going back to school to finish my associate's degree in Tennessee while I'd have a basecamp. Mom sounded great over the phone, and I was excited at the idea of her getting better and taking care of her mental health. She told me that she missed me. It seemed that her long term stay at the facility in Alabama had really helped her. I told her that I would call again soon and update her along the trip.

That following week, I received a package in the mail at my uncle's house. It was my passport that I'd applied for prior to leaving Tennessee. I'd almost forgotten about it. It was dated for September 1st, which lit my heart aflame. My mammaw's birthday was September 1st, and good things always happened on that special day each year. I felt warm inside and looked up to the sky with smiling eyes.

The next morning, I got a text from Luke. He asked if I wanted to go to the Million Dollar Cowboy Bar for lunch that afternoon in Jackson to meet in person.

I sighed and texted him, "I'm actually on my way to Canada."

9

Glaciers

With the radio turned up as far as the dial would go, we were Canada bound! I had dreamt of going to Alberta and British Columbia for as long as I could remember. In my down time back in the days working at the lab, I'd religiously skim my Canada travel book for trip ideas. The Merc was running like a steed. I called Dad on the way up. He wasn't pumped at the idea of me going out of the country alone, but I reassured him that I had the dogs for protection. They made the best traveling companions and were down for anything!

I took the highway route that led us up through Montana so we could check out Glacier National Park. On the way, we passed an exit for a town called Anaconda Opportunity. I thought to myself, *No thanks, but thanks for the opportunity.* There was a lot of time to just think on the road. It was the kind of thinking where I thought to the end of my mind's capacity, and then inspiration poured out effortlessly. Though company was often welcomed, it was nice to jam out to my own playlist.

I pulled the Merc into Glacier National Park and onto Chasing the Sun Road. What a brilliant name for a road. I cruised along the winding curves of abstract pavement to wooded trees through unfamiliar mountains. I had an epiphany. *Chasing the sun—that's what it's all about,* I thought. *Trying to witness all of the world's natural beauty before the sun goes down. Hoping to see as much of these natural wonders in the world before our clock runs out.* What a pure moment it was. I drove around the next bend, and Goose Island appeared right before my eyes! Chris had told me a story about this place one night in the canned ham camper.

A woman, whose tribe lived on the banks of Saint Mary Lake, would swim out to an island every day to escape the loud bustle of her community. One day, she stumbled upon an unexpected visitor. A man, from a tribe on the opposite bank, had been swimming out there to find peace, too. The two fell in love and would swim out in secret every day before sunset. They decided to marry, but both tribes both forbade it. The woman's people told her if she were to meet with the man again, she would be banished. The man continued going to the island and wondered where his lady had gone, thinking she did not love him any longer. He waited there every day until sunset before going back to his tribe. One day, the woman swam with all her breath back to the island, and the man was still there waiting for her. She told him her tribe was going to forbid her return, and he said his tribe had found out their secret, too. That night, they both stayed throughout the sunset with no intent to turn back. The following morning, members of both tribes rowed out to the island to capture their traitors, and no one was there to be found. Only two geese footed nearby, giving each other morning baths in the glistening lake at sunrise.

As I observed Goose Island, I could see this entire story play out in my imagination. After a few deep breaths, I skipped a rock out into the pristine lake and watched the water ripple. Then, I knew it was time to continue along the drive up a steep grade to Logan's Pass. I'd read about a cool hike up there that led to great views of the surrounding glacial peaks. The dogs were not allowed on the trail, so I left them in the car with the windows cracked. It was quite chilly out, so I didn't worry about them getting hot.

I hiked for over a mile up an icy trail, and it started snowing along the way. It was beautiful and my first snow of the season. I reached the top of the trail that overlooked gorgeous ice-capped mountains. I dreamt about summiting all of the peaks as if I could reach out and touch them. I took in the awe of this timeless national park and imagined settling there, if only for a moment. These were serious mountains of the Wild West. I wanted to bask in their glory forever but knew I needed to get back to the pups.

I hustled back down the trail, fully covered in snow by now, in my Chaco sandals and socks. The trees were glazed white, and the thick snowflakes gracefully fell right before my eyes. Everything was so pretty; I took my eyes off the trail for a moment in a winter bliss. I tripped and slid down the trail, jolting the point of my knee into a jagged boulder. I went to pick myself up and blacked out, falling with my back to the cold ground. I came to within minutes but couldn't seem to stand up. My knee was numb, and my vision was blurry. I could make out two figures walking down from the top of the trail and breathed a sigh of relief. It took a little while for them to reach me. While lying there, I imagined all the worst-case scenarios. I was going to be heli-lifted from Logan's Pass. *This would provide great views of the mountain peaks but would be a very costly ride due to my lack of health insurance. What would they do with the dogs?* I couldn't leave the dogs down there. I had to stand up. Two people came closer into view, and I mumbled something I thought was, "Please, will you help me get back on my feet?" They each took an arm and hoisted me up. A lady and her boyfriend walked me down the trail, and I felt strange and useless not being able to stand up on my own. As my legs warmed, I was able to stand once we got down to the parking lot. My knee was swollen and caused a limp in my left leg. "I slid and hit my knee, but I don't know why I blacked out," I said. They said it could have been from the altitude. I assured them I was fine, and they encouraged me to drink more water. I was dehydrated. I thanked them kindly and asked where they were from. "Saskatchewan," said the lady in a Canadian accent. They were a very friendly couple, road tripping the national parks together. I told them I was headed to Alberta for the first time. The lady said, "Oh, I have something for you!" She went to their car and fetched a map of all the Canadian provinces. I was thankful for running into them.

We parted ways, and I sat in the car for a bit to eat a protein bar. I pulled my leggings up over my knee, and there was a thick red gash engraved right on my kneecap in the shape of an X. *That'll make a great scar,* I thought. *A tattoo from nature.* I had blacked out like that before while out hiking back east, often followed by throwing up and ringing in my ears. When it happened in the past, I hadn't been able to regain normal breathing patterns for hours. I thought that I must be really out of shape or something and told myself to *suck it up, buttercup.*

We chased the heck out of Chase the Sun Road and reached the exit of the park. "Hmm, Canada must be near!" I told the dogs. We took a right at the end of the road and pulled over to fuel up. I called Dad and told him I loved him and that I wouldn't have cell service once I crossed the border into Canada.

10

Oh, Canada

It was my first time leaving my home country, and I wasn't sure what to expect. I felt border patrol anxiety. The dogs were hopping around inside the Merc excitably. I watched border patrol officers empty my car inside out as I sat inside a random building that straddled the United States and Canadian borders. I sat there awkwardly with my United States citizenship documents and seemed to be the only car driving into Canada at this hour. Heck, I had just woken up that morning and decided to go for it without much of a plan, or any plan at all. After asking how much money was in my bank account and how long I planned to stay in their country, the patrol officers said I was good to go. I guessed I'd be there for about a week or so but wasn't against posting up all winter if the universe made it happen.

I loaded the dogs back into the car and started up the Merc. We drove further up the road and passed the Alberta sign. I screamed at the top of my lungs, "Canada!" Finally, after seeing all those pictures in my travel books for years, I'd made it to the land of the Red Maple leaf! Joy flooded over my body like the sound of gospel singers. I smiled in content, looking at the long road ahead. Then, something darted across both lanes in front of the car. It looked like a big cat, but I wasn't about to go out searching to confirm.

We kept on driving into the night, deeper north through Alberta. I thought about car-camping until daylight but wasn't familiar with my whereabouts. I fidgeted with the GPS, and it became clear to me that it wouldn't pick up a signal in Canada. That wasn't something I'd anticipated. I suddenly remembered the map that the friendly couple from Glacier had given me. I was relieved to have a source of wayfinding. As we coasted through new territory, I kept a lookout for places to park overnight.

A news alert came over the static in the car radio, and luckily I could pick up a couple AM stations. There was talk of a kidnapping. A little girl had gone missing, and there was suspicion of foul play and possibly…murder. "Nope," I said out loud to the dogs. Since we didn't see any overly inviting camping pull-offs and with this recent news over the radio, I decided to get off the road for the night and into a hotel. We found a pet-friendly room at a very expensive rate, but I knew it was in our best interest for the night to get our bearings first. I used the hotel Wi-Fi to access Facebook and message my dad to let him know we had arrived safely in Alberta.

My knee was sore from earlier and slightly bleeding through the bandage. I took a nice hot shower and cleaned up the wound. I hoped to get a few hikes in while we were visiting Canada. I lay down on a comfy pillow and researched a route for the next day.

The following morning, I fueled up with a continental breakfast and snuck the dogs some bacon. Feeling refreshed, I limped out to the car with my duffle bag and the pups. We were going to go check out Fernie next, a ski town my uncle had suggested back in Idaho. I thought if a seasonal employment opportunity came along, we'd just stay there all winter.

We strolled through town and passed a sign for Fernie Brewery. Big mountains towered around the downtown village. A couple miles later, I pulled a U-turn back to the brewery. I ordered a growler of their maple ale and sampled a few porters and stouts while I waited.

"Where are ye from?" asked the bartender.

"Tennessee," I said.

"Well, you're quite a ways from home, eh?" he said.

"Yes, yes I am," I said with a smile.

I bought a $5 souvenir while I was there, a wall-mount bottle opener with an engraved maple leaf. The dogs and I explored around the ski town and took an unmarked road up through the woods. I kept driving further, pulled in by the wilderness, and found an inviting trailhead. I parked and got out of the Merc. The dogs and I followed a dirt path through a maze of yellow trees and green firs. It was fall, and winter was nearing. It was a beautiful time to see Canada between the seasons, and there was practically no one around. The dogs sprinted to and from a creek that ran parallel to the trail, taking gulps of fresh water. We caught glimpses of the ski hill as we climbed in elevation. Once we returned to the car, we got back on the main road and kept on driving. According to the map, there was no straight route to get to Banff National Park, which I felt drawn to explore. I found myself at a crossroads, metaphorically and literally.

Option one: I could continue southwest into Vancouver and eventually turn back south to the states and ride on pure luck of finding a job and housing in California, or somewhere along the way.

Option two: Continue on to Banff and return home to Tennessee to buy a shed, build an off-grid lifestyle, and go back to school with a future of travel being more sustainable.

I steered over to the side of the road beside another parked car to ponder my options. A big *something* was pulling me towards Banff. Perhaps it was my deep urge to see Lake Louise and the Canadian Rockies, or maybe it was my hidden desire to return home to check on Mom. As I debated the next move, I saw more people pulling over to the side of the road and gathering at the base of the mountain. I got out of the car and walked over to see what the fuss was about. They were filling up bottles and gallon jugs of fresh mountain water runoff. I ran back to the car and collected all my empty Nalgene bottles. I filled them up, one by one, and chugged a whole bottle while standing there. It was the best water I'd ever had in all my lifetime. It tasted so fresh, cold, and pure. "I'm headin' North!" I exclaimed like a mad woman, with Canadian mountain glacial runoff pouring down my cheeks.

We were officially en route to Banff, and I could hardly contain myself. I made another stop for gas, forever confused by the liters versus gallons metrics system. Soon after, we pulled into a line at the park entrance. As I drove up for my turn to pay the attendant, a sign explained that there was no fee during the off season. We slid right in, sparing any loss of funds.

Around each turn, the mountains grew bigger and bigger. *These are mountains for giants*, I told myself. The biggest I'd ever seen! I wanted to live there and hike every mountain in sight. This was a place for dreamers and hikers and climbers alike. This was a place of magic and big rocks. The dogs were dumbfounded, tongues drooling from window to window in the backseat. They were not permitted to hike in many places here, so we took in the views mostly from the road. My heart pounded every inch of every mile.

I followed my handheld map to Lake Louise, a place I'd only seen in books and magazines that taunted my mountain lust. We got turned around a couple of times but eventually landed in the right parking lot. The dogs were allowed to get out of the car there since it was a paved walkway. We followed a path that went through a dense bunch of trees and opened up to a breathtaking view of the landmark turquoise lake. Being there in person surpassed any picture, book, or internet search. It was positively stunning, something everyone should see in a lifetime. The snowcapped mountains reflected in the water as if to paint the lake below them in hues of blue triangles. You could toss a rock out into the lake to ripple the image, and it quickly regathered itself. These mountains were real life.

We hung out for a while, and I was captivated, in awe of the snowy peaks that fed into the glacial lake. I studied the map a bit more and saw signs for Moraine Lake. We hadn't planned to go there, but it seemed we should see it while we had the chance. We got back in the car and followed the winding road, gaining a good chunk of elevation along the way. We reached the top parking lot and took in a deep breath of fresh mountain air. We walked up the path and hopped over a few logs to a stunning panoramic view of Moraine Lake. The mountains filled my soul with peace, and the dogs sipped some water that had flowed from the snowy peaks above.

We descended the road from those two stunning Canadian lakes and pulled the map back out. Our next big marker was Calgary, and we'd go from there.

It was about a two-hour drive. Night began to fall. We were low on gas and still trucking along. We came upon an exit sign and took the ramp to a town I'd never heard of. Canmore. It should have been called *Can-of-More Badass Mountains*. I pulled around to a lodge parking lot, and even in the dark, I could tell these mountains must have stood as tall as the sky. These, too, were mountains made for giants. Standing outside, I had to tilt my head backward and look straight up to see the top of their jagged white peaks, hidden in dark mysterious fog. *Where am I? And where have these big rocks been all of my life?* I felt like I had witnessed Heaven itself and would never be the same again. Mountains like those haunted me. I craved conquering them to conquer myself, to replace ideals of beauty and strength, and to journey into the deep, dark unknown. I admired the peaks one final time in solemn respect and returned to the Canadian highway. I was being tugged home to Tennessee.

We skimmed past Calgary in a blur of buildings and lamp streetlights. Before I knew it, we were driving through Saskatchewan. The open road was calling, an idea born from a sketch in San Fran was churning in my mind, and my heart was leading us south. We drove through the flat hills of Saskatchewan and down across the border and into the Dakotas. I had lost how long we'd been on the road, but I couldn't stop driving. It had been at least over a dozen hours when I realized the city of Fargo was practically on the way. We made a quick detour and put Fargo into the GPS. I was a longtime fan of the classic film and couldn't pass up the opportunity. Driving through the dark early hours of the morning, I grew deliriously tired. My eyes were getting heavy. A couple deer ran in front of the semi-truck several miles ahead of the Merc, and I watched it swerve into both lanes. So, I decided to stop at a cheap motel in Fargo.

"American Girl" by Tom Petty came on and woke me up enough to sing at the top of my lungs coasting down the freeway. We pulled into Fargo, and it was just as eerie as the movie. Everything was dark, and the roads were all under construction. We pulled into a gas station, and I grabbed coffee and snacks. I decided to keep driving. Tom Petty had lifted my spirits. The dogs stretched their legs, and I made a friend with the gas station attendant. She asked what we were doing up so early, and I told her we were on a cross-country road trip.

She said that she'd thought about leaving her hometown and seeing what else was out there. I told her to go for it. She smiled and said, "Safe travels."

We were getting close to Chicago. There was toll after toll after toll, and it crossed my mind to stop and find a deep-dish pizza somewhere. Regrettably, I pushed forward until I was out of the city traffic to find a rest stop. My eyes were bloodshot. I let the dogs out to potty, then put up the window deflectors. I leaned the seat back and passed out for three hours, even though it was mid-day. When I woke up, I had enough energy to press onward. We were just shy of 10 hours from East Tennessee.

A few hours into the drive, I completely lost steam. *Just four more hours*, I told myself. Though I didn't have anywhere concrete to go home to, I was de-termined to get back and find a shed to buy and put on my grandfather's land. The minutes were creeping by. I was swerving and knew it was time to get a good rest. We found a cheap hotel and stopped to get a full night's sleep.

11

Tiny House Life

I passed the welcome sign for Tennessee. The rolling hills were nice to see after a time away. The landscape welcomed me home with lush, green, bushy trees and backdrops of Blue Ridge Mountains. Nowhere else in the country had mountains like ours in Appalachia. I nodded a silent hello to my home state, and it felt good to be back with a plan.

Driving through rural Greeneville, I was 30 minutes away from my grandfather's house, where I'd see my mother for the first time since Alabama. I was nervous. She had sounded much better when I'd spoken with her over the phone, and she'd told me to come home. I stopped at the grocery store to grab a snack, procrastinating a bit, and ran into an old buddy from grade school. Yep, I was back in my hometown.

I called Mom to let her know I was close. She sounded excited. I pulled up the familiar long driveway of my grandfather's and instantly smelled cow manure. Back home in the countryside of Bowmantown, this was where I grew up. Mom was standing outside waiting and ran up to the car. I got out, and she hugged me tightly. I felt a bit standoffish towards her, unsure of what to expect.

"How are you doing?" I asked.

"I'm alright and so glad you're home!" she said.

She helped me bring my bag in as the dogs ran around outside. I went into the house and greeted my pappaw. I hadn't been back to that house in a while and saw it as a new beginning.

My pappaw said I could put the shed at the bottom of the hill on his property. He already had electricity wired to one of his storage buildings there, and the yard was flat. I agreed to pay my share for electricity and water and reaffirmed I only planned to stay there long enough to save up for an acre of my own land. He said I could use the shower and kitchen inside the house since I wouldn't have plumbing immediately. There was fresh well water straight from the pump at the top of the hill, and I would use that for drinking water. I always thought it tasted better straight from the well than in the city limits.

Mom was acting like her old self, reminding me of the woman who had raised me. The hospital stay in Alabama really seemed to help her out. She was oddly coherent and made full sentences without switching topics erratically. I was looking forward to this new chapter. With Mom doing better, I was confident about renovating the shed into a tiny house basecamp and getting back into school. I was just relieved she was getting better.

Over the next couple days, I went shed shopping. I found a 12x20 size within the first week I was back in Tennessee for $3,500, allowing me to put a small amount down and make monthly payments on the rest. It was a perfect shell with just enough space to transform into a tiny home. I put the remaining funds left over from the road trip down on the building which totaled $1,200. The payments were $150 a month with no interest if I could pay it off in six months, so that was the plan.

Upon being back in Tennessee, I started waitressing at a local Greek restaurant. It was October, and if all went as planned, I would renovate and insulate the shed into a tiny house on my grandfather's land. This would give me the perfect amount of time to settle in for our mellow Tennessee winter months and start taking college classes in the spring. The universe had brought me back to Tennessee, and I was looking forward to going back to school.

The shed was delivered to the flat spot at the bottom of the hill a few days later. My dad offered to drive up from Florida and help me fix it up. He was crafty and always had an innovative approach to fixing and renovating things. He had worked on all our pre-owned vehicles growing up and was always tinkering with pipes, plumbing, and electrical projects. Living in the old farmhouse with him as a kid meant no shortage of maintenance projects. I was excited and honored to start this build together. It reminded me of growing up and doing projects with him, and I always learned something new along the way.

Over the course of a week, Dad and I insulated and drywalled like it was going out of style. He showed me how to install wiring, and we were constantly charging the power drill. We made many trips to Lowe's. We were both stubborn, naturally, as we worked side by side in a 12x20 space. After slapping on a couple outlets and digging several feet down into the earth for the ground wiring, the shed was almost ready to be spackled and painted! I was not a natural like my father when it came to being handy, but I sure loved to paint and make things look pretty! With Dad's guidance, I learned how to put up a ceiling with proper insulation, as we drilled hole after hole and caulked everything in sight.

After about a week and a half of rigorous handy work and the help of my brilliantly crafty father, the shed was complete and flipped into a livable space. The only thing it lacked was plumbing, which I figured we could add in once I had purchased land to prevent damage during relocation.

Dad headed back south to take care of my grandparents down in Florida. Mom said she was glad I was home and even happier that I was going back to school. It was nice to feel that kind of emotional support from her. I worked doubles at the restaurant and saved every dime I could. Mom walked down to the shed to hang out every now and then before or after my shifts. It was kind of fun to hang around her again, and I was letting my guard down slowly. We talked about life, kind of like we used to. I told her stories from my road trip and asked for her thoughts on traveling the world. She always had a spontaneous adventurous side to her. Every once in a while, during our conversations, she got off topic with a skewed reality, but she was mostly in good spirits. She did mention seeing aliens from time to time, but that was tolerable in comparison to how her mental state had been prior to Alabama.

I bought a full-size bed and painted the interior walls of the shed burnt orange and brown in the spirit of Thanksgiving. I was thankful. The renovation had turned out better than I imagined. It was the perfect size for the dogs and me. I decorated it with maps of my favorite national parks and a bookshelf to host all of my travel books. The sketch of my tiny house had become a reality. I nailed up my maple leaf bottle opener souvenir from the brewery in Fernie and plopped down onto a freshly quilted bed. It was nice to have a place of my own to rest and reflect on summertime travels. I stared at my travel books and reminisced on my time in Canada. Everything was coming together, and I started to feel settled just in time for a Tennessee winter.

12

Unsettling

One night after work, Mom introduced me to her new friend, Diane. She had met her at the neighbor's house earlier that summer. The girl was my age, and I instantly got a strange vibe from her. She was always asking my mom for money and cigarettes. Mom said that Diane was like a daughter to her and had been there for her while I was away. I tried not to judge her without getting to know her more. I was working a lot and came home to sleep and let the dogs outside. Diane started coming around more often and staying at my grandfather's house overnight with Mom.

To my knowledge, Mom had been taking medication since leaving the hospital in Alabama. She went out of her way to ask how my day was and made an effort to have dinner together once a week or so, which was a change from before. She acted differently when Diane was around, though. She wanted someone to hang out with her 24/7 and didn't understand that I had to work and couldn't always be home to entertain her.

Diane was a bad influence on Mom, and I felt uncomfortable around her. She encouraged Mom to drink whiskey while taking her meds, whereas Mom never drank much before. Her medication started going missing when Diane was there, and it led to Mom having terrible withdrawals. She appeared to be shaky and sweaty in the evenings. She said she'd feel shocks throughout her entire body. My gut told me that Diane was stealing her meds, but Mom didn't like it when I accused her. She was very protective of Diane, her "other daughter." They hung out nearly every day, and I kept busy working toward my plan to purchase land. I knew that living there was temporary and could sense things going downhill. Mom had been doing so good at taking better care of herself. Yet, with Diane around, she was starting to slip and grow more paranoid of her surroundings. It was difficult to watch, and I felt helpless.

I insisted to Mom that she couldn't trust Diane to be her friend. She was stealing Mom's medication and who knew what else. Mom started asking me to borrow money. I bought her some food and would take her where she needed to go, but I refused to give her money to drive Diane around and buy her cigarettes. Mom had given me money from time to time growing up, and I didn't mind helping her in return, but hoped she would be more responsible. Soon, she stopped taking her medication altogether and started acting very *off*, again. Diane was bringing a bad crowd around my grandfather's house, and I started to worry for all our safety.

When Mammaw was alive, the house was a safe place for everyone in the family. It was where we all gathered for holidays and retreated to when the world spit us out. She always knew the right things to say to comfort us and had created a home where we could all land in times of uncertainty. I had grown up spending many days and nights at Mammaw's house while my parents both worked full-time. I rode the bus there after school until my dad picked me up on his way home from work. It had become like my home, too. Mammaw had filled that house with so much love and endless home-cooked meals and her presence.

Pappaw, bless his heart, had let the house turn into a very sad place after Mammaw's passing. Mom, in her ill state, had misplaced dishes and forgotten where things went that were once kept tidy in their place. She had always been a very clean and tidy person growing up, fussing at me if a sock went unmatched. When her mental illness had taken over, her cleaning habits changed along with the way she took care of things. The house turned upside down and didn't even seem like it was in the same dimension of time and space as when Mammaw was alive. She would have never let the house become an unsafe, dirty space, especially for family.

13

The Jungle

I began staying at my friend Ren's apartment on the weekends when I didn't work. I felt increasingly uncomfortable around Mom and Diane and had already committed to going back to school. It was early winter, and I was enrolled at the local community college and needed to keep focused on my studies. An old boss of mine contacted me about working for her again at a weight loss clinic in town. I accepted her offer, as she was willing to work around my school schedule and give me full-time hours with decent pay.

Ren and I had known each other since grade school and played basketball together for years. She had been my friend long enough to see Mom's health decline. I cleaned her house and helped with the bills when I stayed over. Mom was getting roped into a new crowd of Diane's friends, and her mental health began to steadily decline once more. I was overcome with guilt. I wanted to help her get better, and I worried about her being there alone with those people. They had all created a hangout area out back near my grandfather's tool building. My pappaw kept to himself in the house and didn't like being bothered by anyone. He used to talk nonstop about politics, traveling West, and his love for cacti, but after the stroke, he mostly kept to himself.

School started. Between that and work, my time for doing much else was limited. I called Dad to vent about Mom's mental state. He was busy taking care of my grandparents, who were aging, and didn't know what to say about Mom anymore. None of us did, and with this new addition of sketchy friends around, I had to protect myself.

It felt comforting being back in school. I always loved going to school and challenging myself with new learning opportunities. Math had been my favorite subject in elementary school, though as I matured, I enjoyed philosophy, sociology, and the arts. I enjoyed learning about new cultures and the evolving human mind. I especially enjoyed learning about paradigm shifts and theories within relation to self, nature, and the environment. I was serious about completing my degree this time and took the max load of classes I could. While I was busy in school, my mind didn't have as much time to wander off to thoughts about Mom.

Wanderlust seemed to always be tap dancing in the back of my mind, though. I found myself studying in the school library and looking up flights to Ireland between subjects. I had long dreamt of going to Ireland. Ancestors on my father's side had roots in Ireland and Wales, and much of our heritage traced back to Celtic culture. Something about the ancient green countryside, dark smooth beer, and Irish accents called to my soul. I had to go. My Ireland travel books sat right beside Canada on my bookshelf back in the shed.

I pondered on the idea of going there for the summertime. Nothing was holding me back but the dogs. The shed plan seemed unstable with Mom acting out, and I couldn't rely on living there to save up for land with her new friends coming and going. The career potential in my hometown was sparse even for folks with their college degrees, and I didn't want to get stuck there. The thought of graduating, paying all my income into rent, and not affording to buy land or travel made me feel trapped. Regardless, I'd still committed to getting my degree. I just needed to resign from the shed plan and forge a new direction.

I found a cheap roundtrip flight from Orlando to Dublin and booked it from the school library computer. I felt safe having an escape plan, far away from my mother. Come June, I would spend a month backpacking the Irish countryside. This gave me motivation to get through the next few months of long school and work hours and to treat myself for making good grades. After-all, I had promised my grandpa I'd make straight As. It also gave me time to figure out dog sitting options by summer.

I started staying with Ren through the week and going back to the shed on weekends. Her apartment was close to where I was taking classes at the local community college. I wanted to stay away from where Mom was as much as possible but needed a place of stability for the dogs. The 45-minute drive to the shed before and after work was eating gas. Mom was having traffic up and down the hill all night, and I couldn't get rest for work or school staying there. She began inviting people over that she was meeting online, and it felt increasingly unsafe. These people she met took advantage of her poor mental state by asking her for money for made up causes. She thought at one point she was sending money to Johnny Depp to help him out of a bind. These strangers would come over and hang out back in my pappaw's tool shed, and he never had any idea who was there or who wasn't. I had a deadbolt lock on my tiny home door and left a light and radio on for the dogs while I was gone to work.

Ren knew that leaving the dogs down there worried me sick. She was so kind to let me start bringing them over to stay at her apartment while I figured out new living arrangements and kept up with my school assignments. I slept on her couch and started paying rent. I kept the apartment clean, and we took turns making dinner. We watched season one of the *Fargo* series together and jammed in her apartment. She had a music room, and we were always writing some kind of music together.

I was thankful to have good friends at work who listened to me complain way too much about my mother. I thought I could help her, but it was wearing me down. I went to work stressed. My boss was like a mother figure, with two daughters of her own that were my same age, and we'd known each other for several years. She had started as my manager and now owned her own business. We grew close during our time working together.

Ren had family in town, and I didn't want to crowd her space. So, I went back to stay at the shed for a week. Mom was much worse. She was having old men over whom she had just met online. She'd meet them on Facebook, send them my pappaw's address, and invite them over to "soak" in her hot tub. It was strange, and I had to remember that she wasn't thinking clearly for herself or her own safety. Trying to talk sense into her was like arguing with a pile of bricks. I thought coming back to Tennessee and staying near her would be a place to land on my feet. And, I had been low key excited at the idea of her mental health improving. She always took good care of me when I was little and made sure we were safe. It was hard to accept this part of her was gone.

A friend invited me out to a concert in Asheville one night while I was staying back at the shed, and I thought it'd be nice to get away. All my schoolwork was caught up, and I needed a break. I couldn't find a sense of safety staying in that shed since Diane had started coming around. The house had become a distant memory of a place I grew up in, and none of it made any logical sense to me. I took the dogs on a quick hike that afternoon before we left. Then, I met Clay in town at a gas station to carpool to the concert. I rode up to Asheville with him and two other friends. Everyone seemed ready for a night out. We picked up some beer and pregamed the drive up.

We walked into the Orange Peel, a favorite Asheville music venue, to some dubstep show playing loud beats. This part of the city felt like a home away from home, a familiar comfort space. I was feeling the music and the evening and wanted to rid my mind of any thoughts of my mother. I made great friends with a girl named Bre, whom Clay had introduced me to. We danced and grooved and even took pee breaks in the girl's bathroom together.

On our last trip to the bathroom before the next set, Bre said, "Do you want to have the best night of your life?"

And I said, "Of course!"

She said, "Take this," and handed me a white pill.

"Aspirin?" I asked.

"You're cute. It's ecstasy, doll," she said.

The music had been just right all night, and I swallowed it with a big gulp of water. We went back to the dance floor and moved in sync until the show was over and the last call was announced. We hugged a lot. All the music and lights faded into long stretches of colors and sounds, and time seemed to warp. Bre and I met the guys back at the car. They'd been invited to an after party, and so the night swept us away. We pulled up to a seven-story hotel. It was much nicer than what I'd expected for an after party for big kids *our age.*

We rode the elevator up to the fifth floor and knocked on the door. With four of us in our group, we walked into the most chill and relaxing environment. I could feel the tension from the last few weeks melt off my shoulders immediately. Vibes were low key, and everyone was calm and smiling, conversing among longtime friends over music. A beautiful dark-skinned lady walked over to me and said, "Welcome to our room. My name is Coral." She had luscious afro curls and more soul than a hole-in-the-wall jazz club. We hugged, and she pulled me around to meet everyone. I don't remember anyone else's name, as she was obviously the star of the show.

I noticed a few people taking turns at something hunched over the hotel dresser. Coral caught my stare and said, "Oh, come here!" I went and sat beside her, and she handed me a rolled-up dollar bill. "Thank you," I said. She laughed angelic, and said, "No, silly," pointing to a white line of powder on the dresser. "Oh," I said. I had never done cocaine before. She was so politely convincing with her dark rosy cheeks and bouncy hair, and I accepted her invitation. I leaned over and took my first sniff of pure cocaine. "Whoa," I said. Though the room had already seemed calm and serene, everything started glowing. I could see peace steaming off Coral's bare shoulders, her smile wide and gentle. Bre sat behind me giving my neck a deep, much needed massage. Clay laughed, knowing it was my first go, and said, "She's in for a surprise." And boy, was he right.

Coral tossed her head back in graceful laughter. I saw jungle trees surrounding her, as she stood in a rainforest that was the hotel room on the fifth floor. The people that sat nearby were her pet tigers, and a warm rain drizzled down her rosy cheeks until she asked it not to. I stared in awe as a vibrantly colored Toucan flew behind her. "Come on, Millie," Clay tugged at my shoulder. It was time to go, and I hugged Coral once more and wished her well on her journey in life. I found it unlikely I'd ever see her again.

Clay drove us back to Johnson City. I wasn't the least bit tired, though, and I never went to bed. I drove back to the shed early that morning and decided to take the dogs on a big hike. I had more energy than I knew what to do with. We trekked three miles up to a familiar waterfall, and I splashed cold creek water across my face. On the walk back, I felt a headache, something fierce along with cottonmouth and wondered if that was how presidents felt back in the day after giving a high-strung speech.

14

Anxiety

The next week, I went back to Ren's and said, "Dude, I tried coke over the weekend." She laughed and looked at me like I was joking. She waited a few minutes then said, "About time. I tried it last summer." I couldn't believe she had tried it and never told me. We talked about our new life experiences over a marathon of *Fargo*. The dogs stayed the night with us in her apartment, and I was relieved to be anywhere but the shed down at my grandfather's.

I loved living in the shed and was so proud of the way it had come together with Dad's help. It was simple and only held the things I needed. There was just enough room to sleep, cook, and keep a bookshelf and a small moveable closet. It was just how I'd imagined it in my journal back in San Francisco at Mako's. The downside was inarguably the location and the environment. I had put myself in a predicament, with a false hope that things would feel like they used to. I owned my mistake, now what? Mom's welcoming demeanor had changed greatly from when we'd spoken on the road, and Diane was a ticking time bomb.

Another couple weeks of school and work passed by. It was getting closer to May, which meant one more semester nearly down. Ren and I were getting on each other's nerves, which was typical for the cycle of our friendship. I went back to the shed on and off to give her space. I stayed motivated in school with thoughts of Ireland. Dad agreed to keep the dogs while I was away, and I looked forward to venturing off to uncharted lands and getting back out of my hometown. I hung waterproof maps of the Irish countryside along the walls inside the shed and studied them each time I was in there.

Mom was getting worse, and I could feel it all going to hell. She was still hanging out with Diane. I avoided them and kept to myself at the bottom of the hill. I was scared someone was going to hurt her, and a big part of me wanted to stay close to protect her. I'd only go up to the house to use the bathroom and take showers. I tried to check in on Mom, where she stayed out back when her friends were over. It was awkward and uncomfortable being around people I knew were taking advantage of her. She would always stick up for them and get ill with me if I spoke wrongly of them or tried to defend her. I would take the dogs hiking as much as possible around work and school. It was always a relief to get out into the woods for some fresh air.

Clay and Bre came by to pick me up one weekend to escape for a little while. At this point, I had a few weeks left of school and didn't even consider looking for apartments again in Tennessee. I had no intention of sticking around there with Mom's mental state and felt a familiar urge to run as far away from my hometown as possible. Bre took us over to her house to get into a hot tub and listen to some chill music. I tried to relax and let all the chaos evaporate with the steam. I thought about how people all around the world had much worse problems to work through, and I told myself everything would be okay. Clay pulled out some cocaine. I was stressed to the max and thought of how relaxing that night we all went out dancing was. And meeting Coral.

I tried it again, but this time it hit differently. I dreaded seeing Mom and Diane back at the house and couldn't shake the thoughts of going back there. I wanted to finish this semester in school, and quitting wasn't an option. My class load was heavy, and I had finals coming up. All these thoughts seemed to flood my brain at once. The steam from the hot tub was making me sweat, and I felt my breathing pattern change as I got dizzy.

I went to stand up and couldn't. Clay helped me up and drove me back to the shed, and I was too anxious to fall asleep. I told him I was fine and just needed to be alone, so he went home. I lay there and felt my heart racing.

My sweaty palms clenched relentlessly to the metal bed posts. I sat with my back against the headboard, as he stared deeply into my eyes. My heart was pounding, and sweat poured down my forehead. I did not know this man, nor did I understand his need for breaking into my bedroom. I was frozen with fear, and he had barred the only door that I could escape through. I sat there, shaking, as he circled the bed and taunted me with his stares. His teeth were that of wolves, each one contently sharpened in prepara-tion for the next kill. He proceeded to walk laps around me, never blinking nor removing that insidious glare.

I took a huge gulp for air and sat up in bed, pulling myself into reality from a horrid dream. The nightmares crept in often during those times at the shed, and this one was by far the most vivid. I jumped out of bed and looked out the window into the dark hours of the night. Mom had been parking her car right outside the front door "to protect me from the aliens." She'd sleep in there in her car until I left for work, then I'd deadbolt the door on the way out.

My heart was still pounding, and I shook off the strange dream. I got dressed for work and felt much more anxious than usual. I sat there for a min-ute and tried to catch my breath. A half hour into my drive to work, I pulled over and called Clay.

"Something doesn't feel right," I told him.

"I feel fine," he said and told me to call into work.

I didn't like calling into work and figured it was just a hangover. I pulled into the parking lot, feeling much worse. My heart raced faster, and my face flushed red. I walked into the office, trying to act normal, and collapsed into a chair. My boss walked over and asked what was going on. "My heart feels weird," I told her. She asked what I did the night before, and I couldn't bring myself to tell her I had tried cocaine for a second time. I was scared of losing her, just like I had lost Mom. She rushed me to the hospital, as my chest was tightening each minute. She stood by my side in the ER, and the nurse hooked me up to some kind of machine. I guess they had the shock paddles ready to go with my heart rate above 200. The nurse told me, "Push and hold your abdo-men like you're constipated." I thought it sounded odd at first, but it worked to help slow down my heart rate and to ease my anxiety.

I stayed at the hospital overnight, and the staff ran multiple tests on my heart. The doctor came in the next morning and told me I had an arrhythmia that I'd been born with. My heart would beat regularly, then get stressed into an abnormal rhythm. This explained the random blacking out on hikes like at Logan's Pass in Montana and the time in the 7th grade when I had walked off the basketball court fatigued from my heart racing. I told him I had collapsed on several hikes, blacking out and finding it hard to catch my breath, and that intense stress, like arguing with my mother, had often also triggered this same feeling.

While the cocaine didn't help, it had led me to learning something new about myself. Never knew I had a heart issue. The doctor advised me to stay in the hospital for the week to undergo a procedure to fix my irregular heartbeat. He would use a tool controlled by a computer to perform a catheter ablation and *zap* the faulty circuit closed that was causing my heart to malfunction. I said, "Well, that sounds scary." He informed me that without getting it fixed, my heart could go into this irregular rhythm at a time when I was alone hiking in the mountains with nobody to bring me to the ER. This had me convinced enough, and I scheduled the procedure to be done later the following day.

I called Dad and told him what was going on. He was concerned, and I told him that everything was going to be fine. It was a common procedure. He said, "I'll be on my way ASAP," and planned for my aunt to stay with my grandparents. I was pretty worried about undergoing the procedure, because hospitals and doctors freaked me out. I asked him not to tell Mom, because she would add to my stress and was not doing well. I didn't want her in that tiny hospital room talking to the voices in her head, but he insisted that she needed to know. The last he saw her was when we were working on the shed, when she *seemed* to be doing better. My face flushed hot, as I heard her voice outside of the hospital room. My cousin, Nora's daughter, had stopped by to check in and bring some toiletries. I asked her to please stay nearby while Mom was there.

"Millie, is this real? Someone told me you're having heart surgery, but I think they lied. You look fine. Are you fine?" Mom said from the bottom of the hospital bed.

My heart started to race, and I buzzed in a nurse. "Please ask her to leave. I can't handle it," I said.

The following day, a nurse rolled me down to the prep room through two big metal doors, where two new characters stood casually in green scrubs. One fella introduced himself and told me what to expect during the procedure. First, he gave me anesthesia through a vein in my hand. I lay there on a stiff hospital bed in the frigid, cold room. The staff had a happy-go-lucky demeanor, as they were used to the routine, I supposed. I started to enter a daze from the anesthesia. The nurses made an incision and connected the metal camera snake and zap tool through my two groin arteries, one on each side.

I awoke on the table to a long, thin tube driving around inside my heart. *Uneasy.* I looked to my left and saw the surgeon and his apprentice steering the camera with a mouse attached to a computer. *Technology is wild,* I thought. I looked from the doctor to the male nurse standing beside me and wondered if I was dreaming. It wasn't painful but felt like a deep pressure driving around through my veins. "There it is!" the doctor said.

I was in the hospital for seven days. Ren stayed with me for two of those days, and Clay came to visit. I told him I didn't want to hang out anymore and thanked him for being a friend. The procedure went smoothly, and my heart was as good as new they said. The doc told me I wouldn't be able to hike for a few weeks for risk of clotting in my groin. They wheeled me out to Dad's van, and we headed back to the shed.

When we got back, Mom was sitting on the steps. "Dad, I can't be around her while she's like this," I said. She still didn't believe that I was in the hospital for the procedure even though she had seen me there. She thought we were messing with her, and I didn't have the energy to play her games. I took a few days off from school and a week off work and went back to Ren's *temporarily.* Dad took care of the dogs at the shed and came over to Ren's to visit during the day. We took it easy and all watched *Fargo* together. Both my groin arteries were swollen with dark purple bruises. They looked worse than they felt, and I was eager to go on a hike and test out my new heart.

Dad and I got Chinese food at our favorite hole in the wall place in town,

China Garden. It was nice to catch up with him over lo mein and fried rice. He had a lot going on back in Florida. My grandparents were unable to drive, cook for themselves, or keep up their house. Dad helped with cooking, cleaning, doctor appointments, bathing my grandmother, and all the above. I couldn't even begin to imagine the mental strife he was going through himself as his parents, my grandparents, entered this new stage of life. I am proud to be his daughter. He waited until I could walk efficiently and headed back to Florida. Ren told me to bring the dogs back and just stay with her until school ended in a few weeks. I took her up on it.

15

Seasons of Waiting

The days passed, and it was time for a hike. Tennessee saw a late March snow in the higher elevations, and I convinced Ren to go on a hike with me to see a frozen waterfall. I tossed my snowboard on my backpack, and we headed up to the mountains. My heart felt fresh and ready to conquer new peaks! I ran up the last section of the hike and felt strong. The dogs frolicked around the trail, chasing their tails in the snow. We were all our best selves on the trail after a long, interesting East Tennessee winter. Ren and I enjoyed our time together, sharing memories of our friendship leading us up to this point.

Finals were here, and I gave my boss a two weeks' notice that I'd be leaving work. I wanted to do my best on all my tests, then prepare for my backpacking trip to Ireland. She was supportive that I was doing the right thing leaving Tennessee again. She said it was time to move on, and it helped me to hear that.

I received a random message on Facebook. It was Luke from Idaho. He'd seen a picture I had shared on my Facebook page about that first hike after healing. He wrote, "I know we don't know each other very well, but I hope you are doing okay after your heart surgery. I think we have a lot in common and just wanted to say that I hope you are feeling better so we can go for a hike one day!"

I wrote back, "I'll feel better once I get back to those Tetons!"

From there on, we started chatting every day. We talked about Led Zeppelin, Patagonia, Costa Rica, dogs, and our shared love for the Tetons. He was living out there seeing those beautiful peaks daily. He'd text pictures of them to me which practically made me drool on call. We got to know each other in a way I never expected. We texted a lot, learning of each other's favorite foods, books, and lifelong dreams.

After texting for a couple weeks, I wanted to hear his voice over the phone. I sat out in the parking lot of Ren's apartment. The phone vibrated and lit up *Luke Calling.* I felt nervous excitement as I answered. He was sitting on the roof-top of his apartment in Idaho watching some cats climb up a tree. He meowed at them over the phone—*goofy.* It was the first time I ever heard his voice, and I confessed it sounded like *home.* I told him so, and he said I sounded like home, too.

I was smitten by someone I had never seen in person. He said I had a deep country accent, and we talked about our upcoming summer plans. I told him about my backpacking trip to Ireland and how it was my dream to trek the green countryside. He was stoked about it and said we had to keep in touch while I was overseas. He was planning to ride his moto around the dirt roads of Wyoming and Idaho "Wydaho" and do some camping himself that summer.

Finals came to an end, thank God. I talked to the office girls about Luke at work during my last week. It was a nice change in conversation. One evening, I was up late with Ren and told her something beyond my wildest imagination. I said, "I think I love Luke." It was all happening very quickly and unplanned. I was giddy and couldn't wait to meet Luke one day in person. I had nearly forgotten about my trip to Ireland as the semester came to an end. I didn't have a set plan after my return from Dublin, so I thought I might as well road trip back to the Tetons and try again for a big snowy winter.

It was the final countdown. I was mere days away from flying out to Ireland! Two of my best friends, who had offered me their couch last summer on the drive home from Alabama, were getting married to one another! I was asked to be in the wedding as a bridesmaid in Chattanooga earlier in the semester and ordered my dress the week before the wedding while I was at work. My coworkers had helped to size me up and pick one out. Between all the craziness, the girls in the office became like family. They told me that I would end up in the Tetons after Dublin and knew I was falling for Luke. I really didn't know what would happen. He was 1,900 miles away.

I finished the semester with a 4.0 GPA and straight As. *Thank you for motivating me, Pappaw.* It felt productive to get another semester finished, and I had two semesters left to complete my associate's degree. I hugged Ren, thanked her sincerely as we said our goodbyes, and went back to the shed to stay a few days and pack. I told Mom I was leaving to travel some more, but she couldn't really comprehend much more in depth than that. Diane had stopped coming around as much, and Mom was out of money and medicine. Mentally, I had begun to dissociate from her.

I asked my dear friend, Sarah, to be my wedding date. We hadn't gotten to hang out much since I'd been home between school, work, and Mom. She rode down to Chattanooga with me, and we stayed for two nights. The dogs came, too.

After a beautiful ceremony, Sarah and I got hammered at the wedding reception. Catholic wedding receptions were a lot of fun, and they had an open bar. I met the whole family of both the bride and groom; some I had known previously but most were friendly strangers. We drank, sang, and celebrated our two dear friends in marriage. We had a dance battle or two, and it was so much fun. I ended up doing a keg stand in my bridesmaid dress while wearing Chaco sandals, *classic.* I gave an unplanned wedding speech praising the genuine love between my two great friends. They were, no doubt, soulmates.

Sarah teased me that night about falling for a guy I'd never met in person from out in the Tetons. With a little liquid courage, I sent him a message that said *I miss you.* A few minutes later, he called and asked me to be his girlfriend. With Sarah by my side, I said that I would love to be his girl! It was April of 2016. I hung up the phone, accepting the challenge to another dance battle, and felt really happy.

I called Luke later when we got back to the hotel, and Sarah drunkenly lectured him about taking care of me. She acknowledged it was different how we met, but she also told me that she'd never seen me so in love before. We enjoyed each other's company and celebrated all night together. The next morning, I woke up in the most comfortable queen-sized bed all alone. I walked out to the kitchen in the bridal suite, and there was Sarah, ass up and face down on the floor in her dress from the night before. My girl. We'd danced ourselves to sleep!

When we got back to Johnson City, I looked up my flight status to Ireland. There was a notification that my flight time had been changed to a day later. On the ticket, it read that if any major flight changes had occurred from the airline, I qualified for a full refund. I put in a request for the refund and decided to channel that wanderlust into a trip back to the Tetons and to meet the love of my life. I called Luke and told him I was leaving Tennessee soon, skipping Ireland this time around, and heading back West!

16

And We Danced

'Twas the night before I was leaving Tennessee to head south and visit Dad and my grandparents in the sunshine state before driving back to the Tetons. Sarah and our friend, Dugger, insisted that we have a bonfire as a proper send off from Tennessee. My childhood friend and old neighbor, Billy, joined us from over the hill. We had been neighbors all my life. He drove us out to the old farmhouse that I'd grown up in, right over the hill from my pappaw's house. I reminisced on what life was like growing up with Dad in Bowmantown. It made me smile.

The old white abandoned farmhouse smelled the same, musty, and the carpet was as shag brown as the day I moved out. I grew up there. The piano that I had learned "Jingle Bells" on was still there all alone in the music room now covered in dust. Memories flooded my mind from room to room. I used to watch *Jeopardy* every night in the living room with Dad, and our faux Christmas tree sat to the left of the old fireplace. Billy said he remembered the old house and all the good times we had growing up out there in the country. I walked upstairs and climbed out my old bedroom window to sit on the tin roof. I used to lay in my sleeping bag and stare at the stars for hours up there when I was in high school. I stood beside the old height chart that Dad had penciled on the staircase wall to keep up with my growth over the years. I hadn't gotten any taller since I last lived there.

We drove back over to the shed. Mom joined us by the fire and said she invited a friend over. I was content to be leaving in the morning. Sarah and I both happy cried about all the memories we'd made over the last few years. We had grown closer after high school. Dugger insisted I ask my mom to dance, so I did. She seemed happy and carefree. I spun and twirled her around the camp-fire. She was my mother and I, her daughter, *and we danced.*

A dark silhouette appeared moving up the driveway towards the fire. Mom said, "Don't worry. It's just my friend, Jesse." He introduced himself and held out his hand. I shook it with intuitive hesitation, and he held on for a minute and looked further into my eyes. "You're the daughter," he said. I nodded yes. He said, "I want to show you something." I had been walking back and forth loading small items into the trunk of the Merc. I said, "Sure, but I've got to keep packing. I'm leaving tomorrow."

He followed me to the shed and sat on the steps without an invitation. I could tell something was different about Jesse, but I didn't know exactly what and kept telling myself to be patient. It was my last night here, and I wanted to end things on a good note with Mom. He opened a notepad that sat mys-teriously on his lap. "Look, see here. This is my latest design," he said. I sat down beside him and studied his sketches. They were very detailed and looked like they had been perfectly traced, though I could tell they were freehanded. "These are good," I told him. There were sketches of lawn mowers, cars, and intricate details of engines. I could tell Jesse was intelligent by the way he had drawn these pictures to life.

"I work on lawn mowers. I mean, I create them out of older parts, you see," he explained.

"That must take a lot of time and patience," I said.

He turned towards me as he continued to talk about lawn mower engines, and something around his ankle caught my eye. He saw me staring at it and said, "Oh, that. That's just a misunderstanding, you see." I observed it further and realized it was a house arrest bracelet. I felt uneasy and walked back to the fire with him.

It was getting late, and Jesse was leaving to walk home. He gave me an awkward handshake and said he hoped to see me again before I left. After he was out of sight, I asked Mom why he was on house arrest. "He didn't do anything wrong," she said. "It was a misunderstanding." I lectured her a bit and suggested she needed to be careful who she hung around with. She said that he lived down the road, and it was right within his parameters to walk over to my grandfather's property. I swear she was a magnet for these types of situations.

I had saved up a decent amount of cash from working at the clinic and didn't plan much else beyond getting to the Tetons. Luke said there would be plenty of seasonal jobs, and I made a post on the Facebook info board asking about pet-friendly rooms to rent with a few leads. The next morning, I drove out to the grocery store to stock up on road snacks and noticed something red on the steps of the shed when I got back. I stepped out of the car and found that someone had left a rose. I felt eerie chills run down my neck to my arms and was extremely creeped out. Something told me Jesse had left it there.

I walked up the hill and told Mom I was leaving soon. I asked her if it would be safe to leave my bed, some of my books, and a few paintings in the shed with the door locked. She said, "Of course, this is your home." I trusted leaving my things, knowing that the deadbolt key would be on my keyring and the shed would be locked. We hugged. I told her I loved her and found myself feeling relief as I turned the key to start the engine up.

17

New Familiar Places

The dogs and I made it to Florida and greeted the fam. I hugged my grandma and tickled her side to hear that wonderful laugh of hers. She couldn't remember my name any longer, but I felt she recognized my soul. She sang to me and smiled a lifetime of happiness. My grandpa was his usual high-spirited and practical self with a wide ear grin and gave me a big bear hug. He asked about school first. I told him I'd made straight As my first semester back with plans to continue my education out west. I was happy to see Dad. He was walking funny, though, and his feet were all swollen up. He thought he had sun poisoning from being out in the garden all day.

We caught up over dinner, and I told Dad I was moving to Idaho right along the Wyoming border within Teton-view. Grandpa immediately said, "Well, make sure to finish school out there. Your degree is important." He and Grandma were the ones to introduce me to Wyoming in the first place. I asked Dad if he felt okay. His ankles looked like small balloons. He said he felt fine and thought they would go back to normal in a couple of days. I hadn't told him yet that there was a boy in Idaho who I was going to meet. Regardless, the Tetons called, and I'd dreamt of living out there since my first time seeing them. Plus, I was pouring over with excitement for my first time meeting Luke in person.

Dad and I took the sailboat out for a cruise, as Grandma and Grandpa sat on the dock watching for the sunset. Luna and Moe ran around the yard and took turns jumping off the dock into the salty bay. I asked Dad if he could keep Moe for a while until I got settled in Idaho. They were great company for each other, and the landlord I'd been speaking about a rental with only permitted one pet.

After a couple of days, I hugged my family and told them I'd call when I made it safely. I hopped in the car and did the "endless wave" until we were out of sight. I always cried watching my grandparents every summer in the rearview mirror when I was a kid going home to Tennessee. Nothing had changed now that I was a little older and driving West. It was bittersweet every time, leaving their magical home on the bay filled with so much love and fond memories. It was even harder leaving with Dad there, but I knew we'd talk often.

I made a road trip out of the 30-hour drive to Idaho. My first stop was Dallas, Texas. My best friend since the third grade, Carol, had moved there from Tennessee many moons ago for a great job opportunity. It took me about 10 hours to get there.

Luna and I arrived, missing our Moe, and Carol showed me around the artsy parts of Dallas. First, we went out to eat authentic Tex-Mex with tasty margaritas, then bopped around the arts district for the day. She seemed happy with her job in the big city and was the first of our gang that had escaped our hometown. We were always going on some kind of adventure together, and Carol was the closest thing I'd ever had to a sister.

After a night with my lifelong best friend, Luna and I hit the road en route to Breckenridge, Colorado. We drove 13 hours and 817 miles to visit a distant cousin on the way to Idaho. It was our next pit stop on the trip and the first time I'd been to Breckenridge. I hadn't seen my cousin since I was too young to remember, and she was so kind to offer us a place to sleep for the night. Susannah and her dog, Josie, walked Luna and me to our very own guestroom. We settled into their cozy mountaintop lodge not far from downtown Breckenridge. We talked about family and life and caught up over hot tea. Susannah invited us to stay a few more nights, but I was ready to be back in the Tetons. I decided to press on with a bittersweet goodbye to Susannah and the snowy mountains she called home in Breckenridge. She made us a delicious breakfast, then it was time to get back on the road.

It felt good to be headin' West again. The miles were flying by. The closer I got to Wyoming, the slower I drove to slow down the time. I was looking forward to spending my first winter living in the Tetons, and I was nervous-excited to see Luke.

The GPS took us down some unmapped backroads as we neared the border of Colorado and Wyoming. I stopped at a convenience store to fuel up. "Wow, the mountains up here are stunning," I said to Luna in the passenger seat. I was a sucker for new mountain ranges even when greeting them from a distant paved road. I added them all to my mental bucket list of peaks to summit as we inched closer to Wyoming.

It was nine hours from Breckenridge to Driggs, and this was the final stretch. I crossed the border into Wyoming and smiled contently being back in my favorite state. I couldn't wait to hug Luke for the first time in person. I was delighted to be returning to the Tetons. Six hours later, my heart was pounding, and I pulled off at a rest-stop to fix my hair. I had bought a new shirt back in Texas and saved it for that moment. I took a deep breath and looked at myself in the mirror. *What the hell are you doing driving across the country to meet a boy?*

I only had a couple CDs in the car, so Coldplay's *Viva La Vida* was playing in circles. There were no radio stations other than pure static and fiesta tunes. My stomach was a pit. I texted Luke, "I am less than three hours out," and cold chills ran down my arms. The good kind.

I made my way into Jackson Hole, the town that stole my heart on my first trip West. I debated just parking somewhere and sleeping in the car for the night. *Procrastinating.*

Finally, I called Luke to say, "We are right over the mountain pass in Jackson."

He said, "Well, I'm ready. Text me when you get to the light in Driggs."

We hung up, and I let out a shrill of excitement. I drove slowly, very slowly over the pass and reached the town of Victor. It felt like every moment in the past year had been leading up to this one, and I didn't know what to do with it.

I pulled up to the only light in Driggs and texted him, "I am at the light." He wrote back, "I'll meet you at the Teton Overlook."

Eeeeeek! We drove slowly around each curve leading up the mountain. "Death and All of His Friends" by Coldplay came on, for like the 55th time, but it was different this time. I turned it up all the way and stuck my hand out the window to feel that crisp, cold mountain air.

"All summer, we just hurried. So, come over, just be patient and don't worry," said the CD, sending more chills than ever across my body.

A single headlight appeared in my rearview mirror, and a dual-sport motorcycle came speeding around me and zoomed in front of us. It was him. I squealed out loud with excitement, and Luna started wagging her tail against the passenger seat. I sped up and followed the trail lights behind his bike. He pulled into the overlook about a quarter mile in front of me. I crept into the parking lot and parked beside him. I took my time turning off the engine and headlights with sweaty palms. It was dark out, and I opened the car door. Luna leapt out before I could grab her. I took a deep breath. She ran up to Luke and jumped up to give him a kiss right in the mouth then licked his cheeks. I walked up next to him with the cheesiest grin. It was really him, the guy I somehow started loving from 2,000 miles away on the other side of the country.

We moved face to face until we were standing right in front of each other. I studied his face, smile, and the way he even smelled like home. He put his arms around my lower back, pulled me closer, and we kissed for the first time. He bent down and unzipped his backpack to pull out a bouquet of daisies and an Idaho keychain. Daisies were my favorite flowers. He said, "Welcome to Idaho, Millie."

I couldn't think straight or at all. *Was this really happening?* We walked over to a big rock and laid down a blanket. We lay there looking at one another under the dark cloudy sky for quite a while with the silhouette of the Tetons off in the distance.

Over the next couple months, Luke and I spent a lot of time getting to know each other and exploring around the Jedediah Smith Wilderness. I ended up renting a room in Victor from a local but only stayed there for two whole nights that entire summer. Luke and I were in love. I got a job waitressing at the local pizza joint above the bike shop where Luke worked. I would go into work at 4:00 p.m., and he would get off at 5:00 p.m. He picked up Luna every day after work and took her to swim in the creek and hang out at his condo. They became best buds. After work, I'd bring home pizza, and we would bake cookies and cuddle. We scheduled the same days off for Tuesdays and Wednesdays and dubbed those our *adventure days*. We'd pack up whatever outdoor gear and take off exploring the mountains of Wydaho.

We made our first official date at Yellowstone National Park and shared Broulim's sub sandwiches and Montucky Cold Snacks on the tailgate of Luke's Ford Escape. Luna rode in the backseat as we searched for bison and went to see the Grand Prismatic. It was a rainy day, and we were not able to see Old Faithful on that trip. We took it by the mile and embraced each other's company. I fell asleep on Luke's arm on the drive back home, feeling safe and at place.

Luke was from Chicago, Illinois, and had moved out to the valley in Idaho a year after graduating college. The Tetons had sucked him in from the first time he skied at Jackson. He had taken an internship with the local bike shop and liked it so much he never left.

We explored a new place every week during those first two months. We'd share a pint of Ben and Jerry's Phish Food back at his condo without worrying about gaining an extra pound, because we were always climbing some mountain or wandering up a new trail. Some nights, we'd sit on the balcony of his condo and look up at the stars in disbelief that we were both living out there in our favorite place in the world.

Luke called on the way home from work one day and said he'd picked up a surprise from the grocery store. I wondered what he'd gotten for dinner or thought maybe a new flavor of Ben and Jerry's was out. He pulled into the driveway and a long, four-legged ball of fur leapt out from the backseat. The pup ran up, excited to meet Luna. She looked at me then back to the pup. She was not stoked. The pup rolled around and chased its own tail, as Luna hoarded all of her toys by the door. "What should we name him?" asked Luke. After a few hours of thinking it over, Luke decided to call him Bosco.

18

Heartbeats

There were magnificent views of the Tetons off the back deck of the pizza restaurant I was working at, and the tips from my customers were great. Luke would come up to visit when he'd get off from work. Things were good out in Teton Valley.

I'd always hoped to spend a full winter in the Tetons and snowboard at Grand Targhee Resort. In the back of my mind, I was still thinking about the whole big world out there. There was still so much to see in such a short lifetime, and the road called to me. In my state of continuing wanderlust, I Googled Patagonia, Chile. Luke and I talked about how we both wanted to go there someday, but I was thinking about that *someday* being in the next six months after saving up a summer's worth of tips. We could snowboard the big West all winter then head south to explore a new country for the off-season. We didn't have any major responsibilities aside from the dogs. My passport was burning a hole in my pocket, and I yearned to explore more internationally since spending time in Canada. It was refreshing to experience other cultures outside the US. Plus, I was excited to have an adventure buddy to explore with, though unsure if we shared the same wanderlust.

We decided to rent a house with a few of Luke's ski buddies in the valley and stick around indefinitely. A Teton winter was more than enough, and Patagonia could wait. Bunking up with roommates was an affordable way to stay in the Tetons and snowboard. And I'd been wanting to put more energy into my writing. I had been writing a science fiction novel based on a wild dream I'd had several years earlier. Luke and I signed a six-month lease and moved into a shared bedroom together with three other roommates and backyard Teton views, which made for incredible sunsets. We took a special trip out to Rexburg to go "dorm shopping," as we called it, and decorated our room with pictures of our summer adventures together.

It was the first week living in our rental with new roommates. One day, I was scheduled for an evening shift at the pizza restaurant and received a call from my dad early that morning. He sounded different, and I could immediately tell something was wrong. He confessed to me, after much probing, that he didn't feel so well. He told me that the swelling in his legs never went down after I left Florida and had actually spread up to his thighs and lower abdomen. I lightly fussed at him for not telling me sooner and said that I'd be on my way.

I called Luke at work and said, "I'm leaving for Florida tonight. I need to go check on my dad." He panicked a bit and convinced me to wait until the next morning. I called my boss at the pizza restaurant and told him what was up. Later that evening, I packed up a duffle bag with essentials.

Luke finished up a bike lesson at work and came straight home. He'd made a few calls to his coworkers and boss. He looked me straight in the eyes and said, "I'm going with you." He packed up a backpack, and we hit the road bright and early at 5:00 a.m. with the dogs loaded in the backseat. We stopped for gas in the valley and took the mountain pass over through Jackson. From the Mickey D's parking lot, I looked back at the Teton Range and said to Luke, "We'll be back soon."

We drove until we reached the never-ending stretch of Kansas, just in time for a spectacular thunderstorm. We listened to The White Stripes and kept on driving. Dad had told me not to come at first but finally accepted we were on our way after I called him from Kansas. We stopped in Oklahoma to fuel up, and smoke poured out from under the car hood. I noticed fluid leaking below. Luke said the radiator had blown. He went into *figuring stuff out mode* at that moment, and I don't think he ever came out of it. There was a mechanic within 15 miles, and we were able to slowly drive the car there. They ordered a radiator from a shop a few hours south and promised to have us back on the road within eight hours. Eight. Long. Hours. I called Dad and let him know that we'd be there as soon as we could but were currently broken down in Blackwell, Oklahoma. *Oh, Blackwell, Oklahoma.*

We got back on the road in time for nightfall and pushed a few hours farther. We decided to get a motel in Little Rock, Arkansas. Luke was excited about the Waffle House, so we had an all-star breakfast-dinner with chocolate chip pancakes and each a glass of chocolate milk. The waitress surprised us with whipped cream and chocolate chips on top of our chocolate milk, which made everything a little better. We walked back up to the motel and realized we had left Bosco out of his crate in the room. The entire border of carpet around the base of the room was shredded. We cleaned up the mess and decided the room looked better without the carpet anyway. I stuffed the scraps into a plastic bag and hid it in our luggage.

We hit the road the next morning and finished up the eight-and-a-half-hour drive to my grandparents' house in Gulf Breeze. My aunt had picked up my grandparents already, and we didn't get to see them before they left. I hurried into the house to see Dad. He was swollen like a balloon ready to pop. I'd never seen him like that. He had really undersold the seriousness of the swelling. From his toes to his hidden ankles up to his thighs and into his lower stomach, he was filled with fluid. I could poke his skin, and the imprint of my finger would show up before slowly fading away. Luke and I went to talk privately on the back deck, and I said, "We need to get him to the Emergency Room, now." Moe walked up to me, tail wagging, and appeared to have gained around 20 pounds from all the treats he'd been getting. It was love at first sight for Bosco. *And now we were a family of three dogs.*

Dad was reluctant to go to the ER. He didn't have insurance, and he did have a very strong will. Meanwhile, Luke contacted his boss and said he would be flying back in a week. Originally, we'd planned to drive back, but I told Luke that I would be staying until we figured out what was going on with

Dad. Meanwhile, Luke contacted his boss and said he would be flying back in a week. Originally, we'd planned to drive back, but I told Luke that I would be staying until we figured out what was going on with Dad.

Dad's swelling condition was worsening by the day and by a miracle, we convinced him to go to the ER later that week. They ran several tests on him in the hospital. From the tests, we learned that Dad's heart was not pumping at 100%, and so, they wanted to keep him a couple extra days to perform a heart catheter procedure.

I went back to talk to Luke. We decided he'd better go ahead and get a plane ticket back to Idaho since we didn't know how long I'd be staying in Florida. He went out and bought a carry-on dog crate small enough for Bosco to ride on the plane with him. He booked a ticket for the next morning and had to get back to work.

The following day, I drove Luke and Bosco to the airport then headed back to the hospital to be with Dad. There was no way I was leaving him. I told Luke I'd drive back out to Idaho once we figured out everything was going to be okay. All of our stuff was back in the rental house in the Tetons, with a few pictures hung freshly on the wall.

At the hospital, they released several dozen pounds of fluid from Dad's body and prescribed medication to keep the swelling down. They said he could go home to rest as we awaited his next appointment. Dad was worried about the wellbeing of my grandparents while in his older sister's care. Dad had been their primary caregiver for around five years. He had refused to let them go into a nursing home and had sacrificed a lot to step into that role.

The next few days were a blur. Dad and I drove out to the beach and took a walk together down the pier. I hugged Dad a lot, worried about him, as we were uncertain of what was going on with his heart. I glared off the end of the pier into the crashing waves of the Gulf. A bright green sea turtle swam underneath our feet, cheering us both up. I couldn't help but keep asking Dad how he was feeling. He said he felt okay, just really tired. We drove around the peninsula to old familiar places, then decided to go back home to rest up. Dad was tired, and I wanted to sleep, too. There was a lot to process.

Dad's nephew, his eldest sister's son, Eddie, and his girlfriend, Priscilla, came over the morning of Dad's heart procedure. They lived a half hour away from my grandparents' condo. Dad was weak and worried about going back to the hospital. Eddie and Priscilla had planned to follow us there and stay throughout the procedure. I was glad, at first, to have family there for support.

Priscilla walked in through the front door of my grandparent's condo without any sort of greeting, then immediately began gawking at my grandmother's kitchen decorations. She said, "Oh, that must go! Those faux flowers are so outdated. Ew." My aunt had apparently been moving quickly on getting her son to the condo and shifting plans for my grandparents while Dad was sick. When it was time to head to the hospital, they asked to stay in the house to look around a little longer. It was an odd request, given we were navigating Dad's health emergency. Dad reiterated that Grandpa wanted the house locked while they were away.

They followed us in a separate vehicle and stayed at the hospital for 15 minutes then left. I tapped my feet anxiously on the white tiled floor, hoping to hear from a doctor soon while Dad was in the procedural room. A couple hours passed, then they finally gave me the okay to go into his room after the procedure was finished. The results of the heart catheter showed that Dad's LAD artery had 100% blockage, also known as the *Widowmaker* heart attack. The doc explained to us that at some point, Dad had undergone a severe heart attack. His heart refraction had slowed down and was not pumping blood sufficiently, resulting in some degree of fluid buildup.

This was a lot to take in. I couldn't believe he had been so strong-willed to not realize he'd suffered a major heart attack. I tried my best not to cry in the hospital room, but tears poured down my cheeks. I had so many questions; we both did. The doctor kept Dad for a few more hours and explained everything further to us, but we were both confused about what it all meant. *Did he have a limited time to live? Would he ever fully recover? Could he live his normal life? Mow the yard? Be able to care for my grandparents?* The doctor said he would call within a week to schedule a follow-up appointment.

We rode back home from the hospital, mostly in silence. I tried to be strong for my dad. He was super bummed out and so was I. I worried greatly about him and wanted him to be okay. We picked up a salad to eat for dinner, and I grabbed a six-pack of beer and a can of Skoal chewing tobacco (a bad habit I'd picked up in Tennessee). When we got back to the house, Dad said he was exhausted and just wanted to hang out in bed the rest of the night. I paced around my grandparents' condo and called to tell Luke about Dad's test results. I wasn't sure how to take the news. It seemed the doctor couldn't really answer all our questions, or maybe we couldn't think of how to ask them the right way.

While Dad was napping, I drove out to a local park near the beach. Everything I Googled said the Widowmaker was the worst kind of heart attack. The breeze felt nice rolling in off the bay. I put in a big pinch of Skoal and took two sizable gulps of beer. I reminisced about riding my bike down those familiar roads around the bay with my grandpa in the summers.

I felt a strange sensation overcome my chest and puked the beer back up into the sand. Something was off. I took a sip of water and figured it was just my nerves from the day. Deep breathing, I sat on the swings under the Florida night sky and tried to take another sip of beer. It made my stomach churn just from the smell, though I usually enjoyed the scent of beer. The dip made my stomach even more upset, so I spit it all out. *What's going on?* I thought to myself.

I called Luke to talk about everything. He was having troubles of his own out in Idaho. He explained that our new landlord was complaining about having Bosco in the house since he was less than a year old. Along with being extra stressed, I was feeling jealous over the girl roommate Luke was spending time with and started an unnecessary argument. We had been arguing a lot over the phone that week, and everything felt tense. I told him we'd talk later and hung up. I drove back to the house and walked in to check on Dad. He was still asleep. I lay there in bed, extremely tired but wide awake for the rest of the night.

The following day, I awoke nauseous and fatigued. I drove out to Walmart to buy a pregnancy test, thinking there was no way I was pregnant and that I was probably just having a silly panic. Something was different, though. I splashed cold water on my face in the bathroom at Walmart. *Pull yourself together, Millie.*

I took the pregnancy test out of the box and peed on the stick, just like in the commercials. After a couple of minutes, a blue plus sign appeared. *Hmm, that can't be right.* I drank a bunch of water and peed on the second stick in the box. Blue plus sign, again. I stared at myself blankly in the mirror. It was September 1st, my mammaw's birthday. Good things always happen on September 1st. This was unexpected. "I am pregnant," I sighed under my breath while holding the stick up to the light.

A blur of thoughts crossed my mind. *I don't know the first thing about taking care of a baby. I just like to travel and play with the dogs and stuff. I don't know how to feed an infant. I've never even held one before.*

"Oh, God…Luke," I said to myself in the mirror.

I went back to the condo and needed to make a plan. I needed to talk to someone and get advice. Not Dad. Not Luke. Not yet. My cousin back in Tennessee had announced a few weeks earlier that she was pregnant. *That's it, I'll ask her.* I sent her a message in a mixed state of joy, confusion, and heartbreak from Dad's news the day before and my recently learned news. She told me to buy prenatal vitamins and to research Tennessee state insurance. It was sound advice, and I was *overwhelmed.*

Next, I had to tell my best friend and get her advice. I called Sarah. She was excited about the news and told me that she had my back no matter what. Sarah was a mother herself, and I was grateful to confide in her while debating how to tell Luke I was pregnant. I preferred to tell him in person, but we didn't even know when we'd be seeing each other next. I messaged my old boss from Tennessee. She was like a mother, and I knew she would know what to do. She was so excited she couldn't stand it. She told the girls in our office, and they told me they would answer any questions I had. They were all mothers. I was freaking out about all the new changes going on inside my body. I had been toning up from all the hikes back in Idaho and now, my future seemed less about being fit. *Big changes. Big hormones. So, so sleepy.*

I had never thought of myself as being pregnant before. *Would I even be a good mother?* I selfishly wanted to travel the world. *Traveling with kids?* I was still trying to figure out how Moe had gotten so overweight in such a short time away. And keeping up with Luna chasing her ball was great, like a walk in the park. *But a baby?* They have such soft fragile heads and need constant attention. I was ill-prepared for this step in life and extremely tired. All I wanted to do was nap, and my boobies were so tender and sore. I was both pregnant and afraid of losing my father. So, I locked myself in the guest room and cried a lot.

I woke up later in the afternoon. My thoughts flashed back and forth from the widowmaker heart attack to pregnancy to Luke's female roommate and to my growing appetite. I just wanted pizza so bad, so I ordered a medium thin crust from Domino's with black olives, onions, bacon, and white sauce. It sounded good at the moment, but Dad said it tasted gross. I drove out to buy prenatal multivitamins since my cousin said it was necessary for the baby's health. They made me even more nauseous.

I drove Dad to his doctor's appointment the next day. The doc had scheduled Dad to have a defibrillator implanted within the month, then instructed him to rest up and take it as easy as possible until then. This was big news. We went to IHOP afterwards to stress-eat together. I ordered a mile high stack of chocolate chip pancakes, and Dad went for the lower sodium options. He was processing all the news about his heart, and I was very moody and feeling sick over all the smells in the restaurant. I wanted, so badly, to tell Dad I was pregnant and scared but didn't want to worry him or add any extra stress.

Luke and I had been fussing about things all week over text. He was worried we were going to get kicked out of the house for having a puppy, and that was the least of my concerns. I missed him and was nervous about telling him that I was pregnant. We had only been dating for four-ish months, and I didn't know what to expect. So much had happened so quickly. I was texting him beneath the table while Dad and I waited for our breakfast in pure silence. Dad and I were processing the news of the defibrillator, which would double as a pacemaker. Luke was messaging me about what to do with Bosco and the house. And I *hangrily* snapped and texted it without thinking: "LUKE, I'm pregnant!"

The phone started ringing nonstop, and I tried to act casual sitting at the table across from Dad. I didn't want to discuss everything right then. I hadn't meant to tell Luke over text and wished I had waited to do it in person, but

I was overwhelmed and couldn't keep it to myself any longer. I called him as soon as we got back to the house. He said he'd thrown up 16 times at work and just wanted to be on the same side of the country, in the same place, more than anything. I was relieved we could talk about it together and try to figure out next steps. The next day, he talked to his boss and told him the news. Luke had decided to take off later that night to begin the 30-hour drive back to Florida.

Dad was glum. A defibrillator was serious business. We drove over to the beach to relax and get things off our minds. Thankfully, most of the swelling in Dad's legs and abdomen had gone down, but they told him not to do any strenuous activity and to continue taking the medication daily. I told Dad that Luke was heading our way soon, but I kept the pregnancy news to myself. I wasn't sure how he would react, and he had enough to worry about.

My grandpa called each afternoon to check in on Dad. Dad wasn't able to take care of my grandparents for the time being, and we were unsure of how my aunt was treating them while in her care. I hugged Dad often and made us a low-sodium ground turkey chili for lunch. He looked at it and said, "What is that smell?" We both laughed and retreated to our rooms for more napping.

Luke and Bosco showed up late the next night. He had driven non-stop until he got to Florida. We gave each other the biggest hug aside from our first time meeting at the Teton Overlook. It was a relief to be back in the same state. We talked about a lot of things over the days that followed: how we were going to tell Dad the news, where we were going to live, where we would go after Florida, and that neither of us had ever changed a diaper before. We went to Zaxby's to think about it all over fried chicken. My stomach turned, and I couldn't eat it. I had formed aversions towards all the foods I loved: pizza, chocolate, ice cream, and now Zaxby's chicken. We did a lot of melancholy window-staring and deep life reflection of how we ended up there, in Florida, with a baby on the way. I tried to tell Dad of the news over the next couple days but failed. I would open my mouth and choke on my spit.

All three of us sat out on the dock to watch the sun go down one evening. I cherished many memories sitting out on that dock with my family, watching the sun go down "sittin' on the dock of the bay." I could tell Dad was swelling up again in his ankles. The stars shined bright that night over the bay, and the air was salty, familiar, and comforting. I loved it out there. We listened to the water swish back and forth and the occasional mullet leap towards the stars only to be tugged back into the sea. I felt it was the right moment and took a deep breath and said, "I have some peculiar news, Dad." He smirked and nodded to continue. Luke got wide-eyed and nodded.

I took another deep breath and said, "I-I'm pregnant!"

Dad exclaimed, "What!? Seriously?" I told him I was not joking.

He said, "Well, congratulations to you both!" and gave me a big hug.

Luke and I went out to a café on the beach the next morning to get serious about future planning. I knew I needed to apply for state insurance back in my home state of Tennessee and find prenatal healthcare. This was an unplanned part of the journey, most def.

We could stay in the shed, *temporarily*. It was about a 10-hour drive from where we were in Florida. Luke and I talked it over. All our belongings were still in Idaho. We talked about going back there to live with our roommates but knew we'd have to do something with Bosco. I didn't know how quickly I could get health insurance there without residency and didn't know who to talk to for support that far away. I was hesitant to be that far away from Dad. Tennessee seemed like the most practical option for the time being, so we decided to head north in a few days.

I didn't want to leave Dad alone down in Florida but needed to see how far along I was. I was ready to get checked out by a doctor. I planned to come back for Dad's appointment in a month to check on him and drive him to get his defibrillator implanted. He promised not to do anything too strenuous or try and mow the yard while we were gone.

Luke, our three dogs, and I hit the road for Tennessee. We left my car in Florida at Dad's and rode up together in the Ford Escape.

19

Seeds of Doubt

It felt like I had known Luke for years. I warned him about meeting my mother. I didn't know what frame of mind she'd be in and wasn't thinking much beyond getting a doctor's appointment to see how far along the baby was. Luke and I pulled into the familiar driveway of my grandfather's house and parked in front of the shed. It was nearing October, and I had left this place over nearly half a year ago with no intentions on returning so soon. "Well, here it is," I said. I had talked with Luke a lot about the shed and my failed attempt to live the tiny home lifestyle on my grandfather's land. I was proud of how it had turned out, though, and all the time and work Dad and I had put into it. It had given me hope to one day own land and travel full-time with a basecamp. Though, now I was to become a mother, and thoughts of traveling full-time seemed long distant.

Mom came down the hill and announced her presence with a thick country accent, "Well, hello there!" Luke was from up north and probably having a bit of culture shock I'd imagined, *playing it cool*. I clenched my teeth, uncertain of Mom's current mental state. Everything felt so strange and warped back at that house, like an alternate universe, *an abstract version of what was*. My mind trailed off, as Luke introduced himself and gave Mom a hug. We sat down on the steps of the shed to ponder.

"Mom, I'm pregnant," I said.

"Are you serious?" she asked. "I'm going to be a grandma?"

"Yes," I said. She seemed excited.

She looked up at the clouds in a state of wonder. She mumbled something about the president flying over us in a helicopter with Johnny Depp and seemed to be in a mostly good mood. We went into the shed and brought our few things inside. My bed, bookshelf, and the crate for the dogs were still in there. Mom had confessed to breaking the door handle to get in while I was away. She had let one of her friends stay there for a night, she said. It really hurt to hear this, and my once safe space felt totally violated. I pushed those thoughts way back in my brain and remembered that I needed to see a doctor. This was a place for us to stay *temporarily* to figure out our next move. *Power through, Millie.*

Sometimes, I'd beat myself up for thinking Mom could change or act like the woman I'd known most of my life. The one who used to give a shit about her child's wellbeing or whereabouts or respected her things. The woman who would have *Friends* marathons with me and binge-eat cupcakes or bake late night pepperoni pizzas. She looked just like that same woman, but this was not my mother, and it wouldn't click. It took me lesson after lesson of trying to decipher who this replica of her was in human form, who looked and sounded identical to my mom but had downright spiteful intentions at times.

I went to the health department first thing the next morning and enrolled in a state insurance program called *TennCare*. I was thankful such a thing even existed, because most of the jobs I'd had previously didn't offer insurance at all, or came with very high deductibles.

I found an OBGYN that accepted my insurance and began with a regular checkup. It was confirmed that I was around 12 weeks pregnant. We had a healthy baby growing. Luke's face was pale, and I was nervous about the idea of childbirth. Ever since I'd seen the movie *Jersey Girl* as a kid, I was terrified at the thought of dying during childbirth. *Going through such a beautiful and agonizing process, then never meeting your child.* I pushed those thoughts to the back of my mind and accepted that a baby was growing inside my stomach.

Luke applied for jobs in the Tri-Cities everywhere he could. He had his bachelor's degree in outdoor recreation and marketing, but the job market around Johnson City was a drag. I contacted my previous boss from the weight loss clinic, and she offered me my position back full-time. I was grateful to be around my familiar work family of loving women who would help guide me through the prenatal journey. I knew this industry, and it provided us with a stable paycheck to get things going back in Tennessee.

We took lots of drives to town to get out of the shed and have space away from Mom. We hung out in coffee shops assessing our next steps and looking up rentals. We wanted to go back to the Tetons, but with me now pregnant, we weren't sure how to afford a lifestyle out there without having roommates. Luke continued to look for marketing gigs, and we researched our housing options. We both knew that we couldn't stay in the shed for very long. Between no plumbing, a growing belly, and my mother, the odds were not in our favor. I would squat and pee outside, and my once-was dream of "tiny house life" now seemed flipped sideways. With three dogs and another adult and baby on the way, the shed was a bit cramped. The travel maps on the wall seemed to have been hung a lifetime ago, and my bookshelf now held Prenatal memoirs, pushing my travel books to the side.

Moe had been acting strange ever since we got back to Tennessee. I suspected he could sense that I was pregnant, along with a lot of changes, plus he'd been getting a lot of one-on-one spoiling while staying in Florida with Dad. Luke and I planned a drive to Chattanooga to visit with my mom's younger sister and her husband for Thanksgiving. I was hormonal, and Luke was stressed about not having a job. Before leaving, Luke went to load Moe up in the vehicle, tugging at his collar, and Moe bit him. We arrived at my aunt's, crated the dogs in the house, and planned to stay for a few days.

My aunt welcomed us into her home. Kay and I had been close growing up. She would always braid my hair for school when I stayed over at Mammaw's house. She was the youngest sibling of my mother, and we had always shared a special bond. It felt nice to be able to reconnect with her, as our family had been in disarray since we all lost my mammaw. Kay hadn't lived close enough over the years to see the full effects of Mom's mental deterioration like Nora and I had. She and my uncle had left Tennessee for better job opportunities long before Mom's mental health had truly begun to decline.

We all turned in for the night, and I was wide awake trying to figure out how we had ended up here. It seemed like we were just in the Tetons out exploring new trails, and BOOM, now I was pregnant and right back in Tennessee. I stared up at the dark shadowed ceiling in deep thought, and Luke's phone kept buzzing. It was after midnight, and every few minutes the thing would go off. I glanced over at the screen and saw he had several Snapchat notifications popping up. It made me feel *uneasy, sick to my stomach.* He was asleep, and I peeked at his phone. The first picture he received was of some girl sitting topless on a paddleboard. My stomach sank. *Who is this girl?* I opened another one, and it was another pic of a nearly-nude female. I didn't open anymore. I looked down at my growing belly and felt like a beached whale. I woke Luke up and said, "What the actual hell? It's Thanksgiving!" He looked confused and half asleep. I pointed out the list of recent pictures of random girls on his Snapchat. He didn't say a word. I ran into the bathroom and locked the door.

The following morning on Thanksgiving Day, I cried a lot. I was so confused and knew nothing about raising a child. I thought Luke had my back.

My hormones were all over the place. My body did not feel like mine anymore. I did not feel like myself. Seeing those pictures on his phone made me sick. I knew he was going through a lot of change, and it was scary for us both, but I had trusted him. It felt like we were in it together up to that point.

20

Loyalty

Dad drove up to St. Louis to be with Grandma and Grandpa for Thanksgiving. He explained to my grandparents and aunt that it would be a few months before he could get back to the normal routine they were used to, per the doc's orders. Grandpa wanted to look at houses with Dad while he was in St. Louis, and they found a few that they liked. Dad told Grandpa that after his defibrillator was implanted, he would come back up to St. Louis, and they could settle there if it's what he wanted to do. Dad's oldest sister insisted they move forward with selling their condo immediately to her son and his wife, while Dad was still between appointments for his defibrillator implant.

Dad went back to Florida, and I took a few days off work to go down for his heart procedure. Luke stayed with the dogs in Tennessee and continued his job hunt. I was reluctant to ride back to Florida with my mother, but since my car was still down there, I didn't have much of a choice. Her driving scared the shit out of me, and I needed to get to Dad. Everything else was a blur. She was in a decent mood for the drive. I think she intuitively knew that Dad needed us, but that could have been my wishful thinking. Either way, we made it there safely.

Dad's procedure took a few hours, and everything went smoothly. Mom and I walked next door to grab an early dinner while he was in the recovery room. It was during moments like those when I caught glimpses of *how she used to be*, so caring and centered with her own charisma. It really messed with my head sometimes, though, and made me question all the times she'd acted insane. I had become so skeptical and cautious with her, not knowing what she'd be like from one moment to the next. A part of who I was had shut completely down and built walls of concrete as high as they would go. I was scared to be vulnerable around her, for fear of how she might react from one moment to the next. Sometimes, it showed up as vulgar language triggered by her past, and other times it showed up as hysterical laughter. Either way, it was best to be suited up in my strongest armor.

The doctor put Dad's arm in a sling and said it would take a few months for him to regain full strength from where they implanted the device. He would need several weeks to rest and recover from this procedure. I fussed at him for even thinking about mowing the yard when we got back to my grandparent's condo.

Mom offered to stay a few extra days to help cook and clean while he recovered. It was a change for sure from the last time we drove down to Florida together. She was doing good for the time being, and Dad was glad to have the help. I was thankful for her offer, too, since I needed to get back to work. So, I picked up my car and drove back to Tennessee, and she stayed.

After work that week, Luke and I took a drive up to Chicago for the weekend. We had been bouncing around quite a bit lately, it would seem. It was time to meet Luke's family, and we'd planned to tell them the news that I was pregnant. To say I was nervous would be the understatement of the century. We talked a lot on the way up. I was still feeling icky from the Snapchat pics and reiterated that I had no problem raising the baby by myself and figuring things out. I didn't want Luke to stay with me just because I was pregnant. He deleted his Snapchat account on the way up there, I guessed as a gesture of devotion, and said he wouldn't get pics from those girls anymore. I was a mixed bag of emotions and really just trying to get my bearings.

I tried to read a book on the drive up but felt my stomach churning in knots. I was so nervous to meet his family for the first time and to tell them I was knocked up. I didn't know how big his family was or what to think about any of it, really. All the extra changes going on in my body made me feel extra anxious.

We pulled into Luke's large suburban hometown, and I checked Illinois off my state bucket list. Luke introduced me to his mother and sister. I had texted with his mother a couple times on the drive up, and Luke had already filled her in about our pregnancy. They were very welcoming and sweet. His mom was excited about becoming a grandmother and wasn't sure what the baby would call her. We took his sister, Nina, out for pizza and broke the news over food. She was shocked by the news and snickered, then said, "Dad's going to lose his shit."

I think a big part of me had become very untrusting of women and who I allowed myself to get close to since shutting down with my own mother. I wanted to be vulnerable and couldn't figure out how to let my guard down. In a whirlwind of nerves and second trimester symptoms, I felt overcome with panic. So, I ran to the bathroom and threw up all the pizza we'd just eaten. We headed back to their house, where Luke had grown up less than an hour from Chicago, and he paced around his childhood home until his dad arrived from work.

"Dad, we have some important news to share with you," Luke said.

My face flushed red as I finally swallowed the gulp of saliva that had been pooling in my mouth.

"Should I go into the other room?" I mumbled.

"No. Millie is pregnant," he said, straight into his father's eyes.

Oh, God. Help. I started to sweat. His dad picked up a wash rag. I'll never forget the look on his face.

"What are you two going to do?" he asked, as he began compulsively cleaning the already clean kitchen sink.

"We are taking it day by day," Luke said.

"You can't do that, Luke. You have a baby on the way. There must be a plan," he said, wiping down the cabinet doors.

He sprayed Windex on everything in the house that night, even on the carpet. I was sweating bullets and didn't say much. "Well, we have to tell your grandparents," Luke's dad said. The next day, he planned dinner for the two of us to sit face to face and tell his grandparents. I couldn't sleep and puked more throughout the night, a mix of pregnancy sickness and nerves. Mostly pregnancy sickness, I think.

The next day, we walked into their longtime family tradition restaurant, and the waiter directed us to a table set for 12 people. "Oh, this is a mistake. We only have four coming," I said. Luke's entire family walked into the restaurant at that time. I mean, everyone—aunts, uncles, cousins, and second cousins. They all took turns hugging us both and introducing themselves in a whirlwind of breadsticks and the aroma of marinara sauce. I thought I was going to barf at the table. Being around a lot of people suddenly seemed much harder than it used to. I was anxious and nauseous. I sat across from Luke's grandfather. We both ordered ribs, and I was relieved that we had something in common. He sat quietly and smiled at me the entire time, then said, "Welcome to the family, Millie." I thanked him, and it warmed my anxious heart.

Luke's family was sweet, outgoing, and obnoxious. Plus, my family hadn't gathered together like that since my mammaw had passed and it was a lot to take in. And given my state of pregnancy hormones and grieving my mentally ill mother, I'd become rather introverted, I found. I grew up an only child, but both my parents came from families of five siblings each. I grew up around lots of cousins, aunts, uncles, and family gatherings. Every holiday, every summer, every week. But after Mom got sick and my mammaw passed, everything had changed.

I loved Luke's mom, and I loved his dad. I just didn't know how to give myself permission to let my guard down and be myself around them with everything else going on. And now, I was a flustered mess of pregnancy hormones and wished more than anything I could just confide in my own mother about becoming a mother myself. It had been killing my spirit for years losing her like that. I had become the Grinch of every holiday and *especially* Mother's Day. Mother's Day had become a stab-in-the-heart reminder that my mom was gone, but not really. The mother I knew was gone. With Dad in Florida and Mom being Mom, I had isolated myself in the mountains on any holiday that felt vulnerable to being around family over the last five-ish years. I saw no sense in celebrating any of it and had found my sense of belonging in the mountains and on rivers and roads.

Fast forward, we went back to Tennessee. I was searching for something grounding in what seemed a sea of uncertainty. I wanted to escape my home-town yet again, while also grasping at straws for anything familiar. Everything was changing and moving so quickly. Mom. Dad. My belly. Luke. *His Chicago upbringing.* We talked about going up there to raise our baby, but it all felt so overwhelming, and I wasn't even sure I trusted him anymore. I just wanted to create a safe space to bring a child into the world.

Luke found a marketing job for a local arcade company. He was relieved to start working again. We had both secured full-time work and had narrowed down a few apartments in our search. The late-night, hourly pregnancy-pees outside the shed were soon to be over.

Mom started inviting that creepy guy, Jesse, over again. While I was gone to Idaho that summer, she said he'd been involved in a bad accident while riding an electric bike he'd made from lawn mower parts. The doctors said it was a miracle he was still alive. Mom felt sorry for him and invited him to stay over at my grandfather's house out back in one of the buildings, so she could take care of him. She put an extra bed out there and gave him a TV to watch. He was in a wheelchair and unable to roll down to where we were staying in what was once a tiny house vision. Now, it had felt more like a living episode of *Jerry Springer.* I got a bad feeling around this guy, especially now that I was pregnant.

Luke went with me to my OBGYN appointment one afternoon. We found out we were having a little girl. I would have been enamored with either gender and felt very excited about having a baby girl. I would raise her to be curious, adventurous, and educated, and I'd always be her life's greatest protector. We had been writing down ideas for names, like Andromeda, Leia, and Colter. I was somewhat of a space nerd, and Luke was obsessed with *Star Wars.* Colter reminded us of Colter Bay back in the Tetons.

Luke flew back to Idaho after we each saved up a couple checks. He packed all our belongings from the rental house into a Budget truck and drove it back across the country. On the way back, he took lots of pictures posing with an ultrasound of our sweet baby girl in many of his favorite places. They were cute snapshots. He arrived back in Tennessee and pulled the moving truck up to the top of the hill, so we could unload our things on flat ground. Jesse rolled over in his wheelchair, while we were taking things off the back of the truck.

"Hidy there," he said. "What y'all got in there?"

"Oh, just some boxes of pictures and things from our house in Idaho," I said uneasily.

He began rambling on about his boyfriend and said that his family didn't like him because he was gay. I couldn't help but glance at the bracelet on his ankle periodically. He told us a lot of things while we unpacked. Though I was only partially listening to his stories about him and his boyfriend, I quickly caught on that he was fabricating all of it. He said the guy picked him up on his electric bike, and they would ride for hours into the sunset. But I knew there was no way this could be true with his house arrest bracelet and wheelchair. His story didn't add up.

My mind flashed from good, safe memories of my mammaw who'd welcome us into this same white stucco house to have a warm home-cooked meal to now—an abandoned, nightmarish scene that felt like ghosts lived there. Jesse went on to tell me that he could not wait to meet my unborn child. It was at that moment I needed to go. To get the *fuck* out of that place, whatever it had become. It wasn't my mammaw's house any longer, and it had taken me a while to accept that reality. We emptied the truck.

We found an apartment online and saved up the remaining parts of the deposit. Mom was hanging out with Jesse daily, and it once again felt unsafe to be around there. She'd say that he was her best friend and not to tell Pappaw he was staying in the tool shed out back.

December came, and we moved into a condo by the lake just in time to pick out a pine tree and decorate it for Christmas. Luke and I decided it was best not to tell Mom where we moved. I didn't want her to show up unannounced or for Jesse to know where we lived. I wanted to create a safe space to get through the remaining months of pregnancy. I wanted to nest and make our new place safe and cozy to bring our daughter home to. We hadn't attended a single parenting or pregnancy class with only a few months to go. I was biting my nails thinking about mortality rates and childbirth and still finding comfort with the girls at work.

I called Dad often to check on him. He was doing okay but still not able to mow the yard, which bugged him. In the interim, my dad's oldest sister filed for power of attorney over my grandparents. Next, she sold their house to her son, Eddie, and his wife, Priscilla. I could tell Dad was disoriented about how quickly it was all happening. I was too. With the house being abruptly sold to her own son, my aunt told my dad to pack all his things and leave immediately. He still had checkups for his heart over the coming weeks to make sure his defibrillator was operating correctly. My grandparents hadn't even gone back to get the rest of their belongings. My aunt monitored their phone calls with Dad and would intercept if my grandfather showed any signs of discontent towards her.

Luke and I offered Dad our spare room in the basement, hoping he would come stay with us. Dad had to forfeit the remainder of his doctor appointments in Florida. My grandparents' condo had been his home for the last five years, and he'd given up his life in Tennessee and a full-time career to become their full-time caregiver. It was what he wanted to do so they could live in their own home where they wanted to be and not in a nursing home or similar-type facility. It was very upsetting to witness how my aunt treated my father and grandparents during a time of weakness, when she saw an opportunity to move her son into bayfront property. She had tricked Dad and my grandparents out of their home.

Dad drove up to Tennessee with a couple boxes of his things and looked tired when he arrived. He had gotten a storage unit down in Florida to put the rest of his belongings into until he could figure out what to do next. We put a mattress and boxspring in the basement room along with a portable closet for the few clothing items he brought up with him. He didn't have health coverage in Tennessee, so he wasn't able to immediately follow up with medical care for his heart, per the doc's instruction. Thankfully, he had a few months of prescriptions written to ensure he was able to keep the fluid swelling down.

Christmas came upon us, and our home was in a state of confusion, change, and sadness. Dad was extremely worried about the wellbeing of my grandparents while they were staying at my aunt's house. I was worried about

Dad's wellbeing and giving childbirth. Luke was settling into his new job. I hoped Mom wouldn't find out where we lived, and the dogs were unsettled amidst a ton of big changes. Meanwhile, my belly just kept growing.

21

Trapped

The New Year had come and gone. Soon, I was to become a mother and Luke a father. We drove back up to Chicago for a baby shower and had a second one in Tennessee the following week. Our family and friends were supportive of the new baby on the way. It all felt surreal and was happening very quickly.

We completed the nursery upstairs at our condo and felt ready for her to be there. We filled it with love, cozy blankets, and lots of stuffed animals. It was the only room in the condo with carpet and had become our favorite space, too. Her closet was packed from end to end with an array of pinks and soft bright oranges. We were well stocked on all sizes of diapers from both baby showers. Luke's mom and Aunt Nina sent lots of goodies from Chicago. We decorated the walls with a mix of our favorite paintings and some cute mountain shelves. I often went into her room to write and reflect on my growing belly in the rocking chair we'd scooped from Facebook Marketplace for $20.

Dad was trying to figure out his next move with my grandparents being so far away. He had entered into a funk trying to get his strength back and fight from a distance to keep my grandparents safe from my aunt in Missouri. It tore me up to see him so down. It took every bit of his energy to walk up the stairs from the basement to access the kitchen, and his heart had not yet regained full strength to do the things he was used to doing. He talked to Grandpa on the phone often, and I could see in his face how much he just wanted to be able to protect them and bring them home to their house in Gulf Breeze. Grandpa would say things like, "I don't like it here" and "Can you come get us?" My aunt was in the process of finalizing my grandparents' condo into her son's name. She even had my grandmother with Alzheimer's Disease sign away her home. I tried to remind Dad that he had to get himself better before he could help anyone else. We loved my grandparents dearly, and it was a tough situation all around.

Moe had been staying with Dad in the basement and became very territorial over the space. I had cut all sugary treats, like Dad had been giving him in Florida, from his diet to help with his weight. But when I wasn't around, Dad would still sneak him lots of treats, as grandfathers do. Moe started growling at Luke when he went downstairs to do laundry. One evening after dinner, we were all sitting at the upstairs table, and Moe was lying underneath in his usual spot. I asked him to go "potty" outside after eating, while he was laying under Dad's legs. I reached for his collar to hook up the leash, and he snapped at my hand with a deep growl. It broke my heart, and I knew he was stressed from all the big changes, like the rest of us. Luke said we couldn't keep him in the house acting like that with the baby on the way. I didn't want to hear that but agreed that something had to give and once again felt *overwhelmed*.

Moe had been my best pal through it all over the last several years, and I was letting him down. We'd been side by side through so much of life and many milestones together. I felt like I was letting everyone down. Long story short and much against my will, I took Moe down to live on my grandfather's property and Mom's word to feed him and keep him safe. It was the hardest thing I ever had to do, to abandon him like that. Well, it didn't last long, and the false hope I'd promised to visit him often eroded when he ended up in the county animal shelter. Mom clearly couldn't care for him, and she was driving around with him one day, where he was taken from her care and put up for adoption.

Moe had been my partner in crime since my freshman year of college. We had hiked every trail to every local waterfall and traveled around the country and Canada together. He had slept at the back of my knees for seven long years of companionship. *How could I have abandoned him? Who was I becoming? What had I become?*

"Wanna go hiking!?" I said to Moe, then a one-year-old pup. He barked and jumped for joy, looking from my eyes to his leash like, "Let's go!" I remember taking him kayaking at Watauga Lake, and the day he jumped off the banks to fetch and retrieve his first stick. He was the best boy in the whole world. And the time he hiked across his first log when we were out chasing waterfalls with tons of creek crossings, as Appalachia had. And all the times I asked him to go "bye-bye," and he jumped right in the truck, or one of my many old used vehicles. He ventured across the country with me and Luna, and they were inseparable. Frolicking on the East Coast and West Coast. He had lived with me for a time at the old farmhouse I grew up in and moved with me from place to place through many stages of life, always right by my side.

Luke watched the animal shelter adoption page daily until he saw that Moe was adopted into a new home. I'd always told myself nothing or anyone in the world could take Moe away from me, and then I had let him go. A part of me left with him that I never got back.

Inside the condo, we were all stressed, and tensions were rising. I was in my third trimester and tried not to think too much about the birthing process creeping up. Though, the idea of childbirth still greatly terrified me. I couldn't wait to hold and embrace my daughter; I was just nervous about the hospital part, the birthing process and mortality rate, and being on an operating table in general.

I started to dread going home after work. Dad was going through a phase where he insisted on trying to fix the gap between Mom and me. I had set a hard boundary with her, and she was upset that I wouldn't give her my home address. Dad pestered me about it often, and I couldn't seem to convince him that she was not good for my own mental health. I could understand where he was coming from in that he wanted me to have a relationship with my mother—the woman who birthed me. He had always taken care of her growing up, even though they were separated. He showed her great respect as the mother of his only child. I didn't trust her any longer since the illness had consumed her, and I especially didn't feel safe with who she chose to hang around. I was trying to make our condo a safe place, a home where she couldn't just break in as she had down at the shed, or a place where she would just show up and call the cops to report figments of her imagination, like at my house with Gilly and Booker. I was about to have this baby, and I couldn't seem to get across to my dad that I didn't have much energy left to entertain thoughts of my mother knowing where we lived or trying to make it all better. I was hanging by a thread.

I had flashbacks of living with Gilly and Booker, when Mom would just show up any hour she pleased. Calling the police and saying ghosts of children were dancing out in our yard. Fantasizing that the president and Johnny Depp would fly over her in helicopters. That aliens ruled the land. Her concoctions of random powder mixtures she'd throw at me without warning (she insisted salt among other mixtures with healing metals were the cure-all and would sprinkle them in my drinks and on my yards and my things).

I couldn't risk these delusional acts at the place where I was to bring home a new baby. I was trying my damndest to create a safe environment, not to mention that we were living under an HOA in one of the *only* affordable rentals we could find in the area. If she showed up acting out, it could cause us to lose our home! It made me ridden with anxiety to even think about her coming around. I pleaded to Dad not to bring it up anymore, as it was causing me so much stress, and I just wanted to be pregnant and find some peace within our home. I felt my blood pressure rise when he mentioned mending my relationship with her. Or any mention of her, really. He had lived out of state for so many years and couldn't grasp all I had been through because of her. I just wanted to come home to our condo and not have to worry about anything other than how we were going to be new parents and raise a baby.

It was never an easy decision to cut Mom out. It broke my heart, day in and day out. There was so much I had wanted to talk to her about and needed to ask her about for motherly advice throughout my pregnancy. I tried to explain this to Dad, because I know his intentions were good. He's a family man through and through, a great protector, but I was trying to tell him that I was suffering greatly because of my mother's mental illness. It brought me such grief that even being near her felt like a primal threat to my own survival. I was in constant *fight or flight* around her. I had to be, to protect myself. I never knew when she would show up with someone I couldn't trust or lash out at me with her imagination. Or cuss me. Or the time she'd put me in a chokehold in Mammaw's white-paneled hallway. It had put me at odds with her, and I wasn't going to risk my daughter being subjected to her nonsense. *Why was I constantly having to defend my position within my own home when I just needed a place to find calm, and peace?*

I rationalized that everyone in our home was going through a lot during that time, but I had a baby that needed me now, and that was my priority. I was terrified Mom would find out where we lived or show up at my work like she had over the years. I was growing tired of having to come up with explanations for my decision to *cut her out*. I knew it was the best thing I could do for mine and the baby's health, but Dad had held onto hope she'd be involved.

22

Go Time

Work was a welcomed escape from going home. The ladies there gave me so much positive advice on what to expect in motherhood over the months to come. I vented to them still about Mom and my fears with giving birth. One of them had a C-section and the other two both had epidurals. I'd made up my mind to try and give birth naturally without an epidural but would sign the paper for one in case of need.

Luke was working out of state occasionally and had no passion whatsoever for his new job. He let it be known that he'd sacrificed a lot to be in Tennessee with me. The closer I got to giving birth, the more I felt overwhelmed by everything. I was having nightmares about Mom showing up again. I wanted Dad to have his own home where he felt comfortable, and I wanted his heart to be okay. I worried so much about him. I missed Moe. My grandparents were stuck at my aunt's house in what seemed an escalating, unsafe situation. My grandfather pleaded to go back home to Florida, knocking over antique clocks in my aunt's house. Then, I continually defended my boundary against my mother to not know where we lived. All the while, I was overthinking worst-case birth scenarios.

My stomach had been in knots since Thanksgiving over that stupid Snapchat ordeal with Luke, and I still didn't fully trust him. I felt self-conscious about my changing body, and amidst a pregnant identity crisis, I'd remembered

Luke telling his dad when we'd first met that I was "usually much skinnier." That comment had stuck in my mind, along with those pictures of the girls he'd been giving attention to around the holidays. I wasn't sure I knew the guy I was having a child with. We had dated each other for less than a year, and I'd been pregnant for most of it. I could hardly remember what it felt like to not be in *fight or flight* mode. I felt so goddamned alone in that condo preparing to enter childbirth.

Soon, I'd be pushing a human being out of my body. I really needed my mom to be normal again more than ever to help guide me through this process of womanhood. I missed her. I longed for her. I needed her to share the wisdom only a mother can share with her daughter. And, at the same time, I was accepting (or trying to accept) that she couldn't mentally meet me where I was at.

I began feeling my gut get uneasy around Luke when we went to bed at night. I expressed my emotions to the girls at work and tried to convince myself it was all the rush of pregnancy hormones. It was a similar feeling to the eve of Thanksgiving with the Snapchat ordeal. I woke up in the middle of the night, and he was asleep. I reached over to his phone and began digging, because my gut told me something wasn't right all those evenings he'd spent *scrolling* on the couch at the condo. All those nights of half-hearted conversation and minimal eye contact were eating at me, as I tried to justify the hole in the pit of my stomach. And to be fair, I wasn't a burst of joy to be around during those times trying to navigate what felt like an impossible sea of shit. The shining light for me was knowing I would meet my daughter soon.

A glimpse through his phone, and I found it. The source of the pit in my stomach that evening. Luke was a very active member of a group chat with three friends he'd known since college. They'd named the group "Dildos." I scrolled through the demeaning messages, one after the next, and seemed to lose respect for his friends whom I hadn't yet met. They shared one nude or near-nude pic after the other in the chat space. They would rate these girls 1–10 each text, and if they were extra "bang-able," they'd get an 11. In the chat, Luke said, "I wish I had the bank account for her" about some girl he'd gone to high school with that became an "Instagram model."

He said these things to his closest friends, while I lay beside him in bed at night growing our child in my belly. I didn't know how to attach feelings to what I was processing those few weeks before birthing our child. I was in go-mode and didn't have the time or energy to entertain this weak circle of boys. My dad had shown me growing up what it meant to be a good man. I felt disrespected. I had become a mother of our daughter, a baby girl, and I didn't like how they carried themselves when talking about women.

I tapped Luke on the back and asked him about the Dildos group chat. He said, "Oh, that's just *locker room talk*." Trump "you know who" was running for his first presidency around that same time and had stated a similar comment regarding public scrutiny over distasteful things he'd said about women. I felt disgusted by Luke's excuse, and I also felt like I could be overreacting again with pregnancy hormones. It was difficult to decipher what was kosher and what wasn't. And regardless, I knew at that moment, I no longer felt an attraction to Luke. But he was the father of my child. Meanwhile, our daughter was growing and healthy, and soon she'd make her grand entrance into the world. And I would forever and always be *her mama*.

I worked at the clinic up until the week before we met our daughter, then would take a short maternity leave. Luke and I went to the final prenatal OB-GYN appointment, and my blood pressure had been higher than normal. The doc said I had preeclampsia and needed to be induced that night. She said to go home and grab an overnight bag then return to the delivery center within two hours. It was go-time. We went to a nearby sandwich shop and spent an ungodly amount on two turkey sandwiches then headed back to the condo to pack a bag. Dad offered to stay with Luna and Bosco that night, and we called Luke's parents to tell them the news. They hit the road from Chicago and headed south to Tennessee. Dad asked if he should call Mom, and I asked him to *please* not do that. I felt guilty for not inviting her but couldn't risk any further stress. I expressed to him about the blood pressure issues I was having and needed to make certain of a calm environment at the hospital.

We checked into the maternity wing of the hospital. The rooms were quiet and relaxing, with views of the Appalachian Mountains right out the window. *This is a nice place to welcome her into the world,* I thought. Luke said it felt like we were on vacation, as he set up a pillow and blanket on the couch in the delivery room. Regardless, I knew he would make a good father. I got into a gown and lay under the covers of the hospital bed. The doc came in and gave me something to "thin the lining of my uterus." We ordered a pizza and set up camp for the night. Luke put on my favorite show, *Friends,* and it felt like a safe place to have a baby. I was ready, as much as one could be.

About an hour later, the phone in the delivery room rang. I picked it up. "Millie is that you?" said my mother from the other end. My heart sank. *Sick to my stomach.* I was speechless and handed the phone to Luke. He hung it up immediately and called the front desk. He explained that under no circumstance could she come into the delivery room. They said there was nothing they could do to keep her out of the visitation area this late without proper paperwork but that she would not be permitted into the delivery room. I tried not to dwell on it too much. *I couldn't afford to.* I hung out in the delivery room with Luke, ate some pizza, and was hopeful for a bit of rest.

The next morning, the doctor came in and used what looked like a plastic crochet needle to "break my water." It felt weird and warmly uncomfortable, like I'd peed on myself. My water was broken unnaturally, and I just lay there in a puddle on the hospital bed. The nurse brought in an egg-shaped exercise ball and placed it under my legs to help "encourage cervical dilation." The nurse had also administered something called Pitocin to help induce labor. Within the hour, I felt the first contraction. *Okay, that was manageable.* Then came another. *Ouch, that was painful.* And then the third. "Luke! Get a nurse in here, now!" I demanded.

I asked for the epidural immediately, and they promptly set everything up and executed the injection into my lower spine. I could feel the pressure of the contractions come and go, but the epidural did wonders. I felt numb from my neck to my toes. I asked Luke, "What do you think Luna would do if she was a cat?" He smirked. I tried not to overthink about the horrific Google images of placentas I had looked up with the girls at work, trying to remain positive that this was going to be a healthy delivery. I was so scared. Sarah showed up, and I asked the nurse to let her in but no one else.

After receiving the Pitocin and epidural, I felt numb from my neck down and an increasing pressure from the contractions. My mother had shown up in the lobby requesting to get into the hospital room and was turned away, thank God. My blood pressure was not stable, and I can't remember if it had dropped since being at-risk of preeclampsia, but it seemed to be an issue. After delivery, my uterus refused to clamp shut, and the doctor took away my baby girl before I got to hold her. I guess I was nearly bleeding to death and received two blood transfusions, while Luke and Sarah held my hands. My body was turning purple, and I just wanted to hold her.

Nurses frantically massaged my lower stomach, and it was the most uncomforting feeling to feel the absence of your baby in your belly after nine months being replaced by strangers (who basically saved my life, but still strangers) giving my abdomen an unwanted massage. They injected something into my thigh amidst the chaos in the delivery room. The doctor asked me if I had anybody I wanted to see, and looking back, I guess she was asking for my final wishes in case I bled to death, fulfilling my most feared prophecy death by childbirth.

"I want to hold my baby!" I exclaimed to her in a rage of everything all at once. After what seemed like a near-fatal birthrate statistic, my uterus pulled itself together by the grace of whichever mechanism—the massaging, the injections, the blood transfusions. And they brought her to me. I looked at Luke, as we welcomed her into my arms. The first sight of our daughter had us both in tears. I smelled her sweet baby scent and imprinted upon her an infinite oath of love and protection as her mother, and she my baby girl. My forever baby girl. She lay there on my chest, my chin softly against the back of her head, my palm ever so gently rubbing her back and her full head of thick hair. What a most precious little angel, my girl, my daughter. And all was well in the world.

Sarah later told me that she smoked a full pack of cigarettes after my delivery. She claimed the hospital room had looked like a bloody horror scene.

Regardless and with all my gratitude, we had one healthy baby girl born on April 24th, 2017. She was the most beautiful thing I'd ever seen. Welcome to the world, Eliza Mae.

23

Changes

It was love at first sight. I never knew something, someone so tiny could make everything in the world make sense. Sometimes, it's difficult to put into words how becoming a mother changed everything. Things that used to matter didn't. Priorities I'd had before were irrelevant. I had everything I could ever need and more. Our instincts as new parents took over. We knew how to hold her, how to feed and take care of her, and how to mold her right into our little family, like we'd studied it our whole lives. The late-night feedings were a welcomed retreat, and she slept so sound in her white, wooden crib. She liked to study the warm lights strung up around the walls of her nursery. And those little mitts, she swatted at me when she was full of milk or wanted to be picked up and held. I was smitten. My heart was still, and the world around us kept spinning. Dad was also smitten with his granddaughter and spent every day loving and protecting and teaching her from then on.

My grandparents were not doing well with my aunt leading their care. A month after Eliza was born, Dad drove up to St. Louis to check on them. He called me once he arrived so I could talk with my grandpa. He wished us a warm congratulations on Eliza's arrival. Dad said Grandma was very confused about her new routine at my aunt's house. I could hear the concern in Dad's voice and had never expected something like this could happen to my grandparents in my wildest dreams. They were so loving and sweet, and I had no idea my aunt could treat them in such a way. I wanted Eliza to meet her great-grandparents, as she was part of them after all. And so was I.

A few days later, Dad called to say both of my grandparents' health was declining fast. My aunt admitted them both into Hospice care at a nearby facility. I still had that plane voucher from Ireland for $500, a godsend. I found a flight for $489 round-trip to St. Louis and booked it for myself and Miss Eliza. Luke was supportive and said we should go, too. Eliza flew for free as an infant on my lap, and we stayed for five days to visit with them.

It was her first time ever flying, and she slept the entire flight in my arms as I stared out over the clouds below. I observed my sweet daughter while she napped and thought, *she was born to travel.* Dad met us at the airport, cheered up instantly by holding his granddaughter. He drove us out to the nursing facility to see my grandparents. I was in shock at how quickly their health had deteriorated since I'd last seen them. Grandma was not eating at all and barely drinking any water, her lips chapped. Grandpa pointed when we walked in and said, "My granddaughter!" It put a teary smile on my face. They were wonderful grandparents and had taught me so much about life and love and the world and hands-on experience through travel.

I introduced Eliza to her great-grandparents for the first time. Grandpa embraced her and didn't speak much after that. He had a blank stare in his eyes, occasionally nodding off. I could tell they had sedated him with medication, something he didn't do while living with Dad down in Florida. I held his hand in mine for a long time. Grandma was still humming and singing like she always did. I talked to her and hugged her a lot. *So sweet, a woman whom I greatly admired and had always looked up to.* I sat Eliza onto her great grandma's lap. Grandma patted her back instinctively after many years of raising children and grandchildren. I was confused how all of this was happening so fast.

My uncle flew in from Idaho, along with my Aunt Amelia from Florida. Our family was scattered all over the continental US, and I'd realized at that moment my grandparents had instilled the travel bug in us all. I felt conflicted over the Hospice care. My grandparents wanted to age naturally, and my aunt had checked them into a place they'd never wanted to go.

I had a bad feeling around my aunt, almost like I did around Jesse, like she had hurt my grandparents intentionally while Dad had been sick in the hospital. I knew they weren't being treated right when they stayed with her. I could hear it in Grandpa's voice. I could see him liven up when the drugs would wear off, but then my aunt would order more morphine on the spot before he could get a word out. I asked him if he was hungry, and he nodded. My uncle suggested that we order his favorite meal, a St. Louis tradition, *Imo's Pizza*. "He won't be able to eat that," my aunt said.

The pizza arrived, and Grandpa got starry eyed. My dad wheeled him over to sit with the rest of us, as my grandma napped on the other side of the room. He gobbled down a few slices, and I swear it lifted his spirit. I tried to feed Grandma applesauce, but she kept spitting it out. I got her to sip some water, but she hadn't eaten in almost three days. Neither of them had seen sunlight since being checked in, other than the small window on the opposite side of their room.

My uncle asked the nursing staff to put my grandparents in wheelchairs so we could take them outside for some sunshine and out of that depressing hospital room. Grandma nodded off and took a siesta out on the facility patio. Grandpa mumbled something that sounded like, "Go home." I wanted to kidnap them both out of that hellhole and take them back down to their home in Florida where they belonged—where Eddie and Priscilla did not belong, as they were now ripping out the flooring to furnish their newly acquired bayfront property.

As soon as we got back inside, Grandpa mustered out, "I want to go home!" My aunt looked deeply into his eyes and said, "Don't worry. You are going home, Daddy. Jesus is calling you home." It felt grotesque hearing those words come of her mouth. *What kind of game was this for her?* My grandparents were not ready to die. I'd just had a conversation with my grandfather days earlier, and now he was so morphined up he couldn't say his own name.

"Grandpa, I love you," I told him. "This is your great granddaughter, Eliza."

"She took her first plane ride out here to meet you and Grandma," I told him.

He stared off into the distance. Just then, my aunt's other son, Eddie's younger brother, walked in and looked Grandpa over like he was sizing him up. "You aren't so tough now, are ya?" he asked. I felt so much anger run over my entire body, then confusion. *How could anyone be mean to my grandparents, the sweetest people on earth who would do anything for anyone?* I couldn't make any sense of it.

Dad and his younger brother reached out to friends of my grandparents who lived in the area. Several people came by to spend time with them that week and shared memories of their time together. I sat by one of Grandpa's old coworkers, as he told me a story of a camping trip they had gone on in their early twenties. It was my grandpa, grandma, and two of their friends. They had gone snorkeling at an old spring in the countryside of Missouri. My grandpa loved scuba diving. The man said that my grandparents were just as in love with each other back then as the last time he saw them. He said they were so much fun to be around and were always off on some adventure or traveling, always holding each other's hands, and raising all their kids together. They had grown up during the Great Depression, and I had so much respect for them and was thankful to have them to look up to. I'd spent so many summers watching Florida sunsets with them, learning to sail with my grandfather, and learning to bake homemade cookie recipes with my grandmother. I hugged my grandparents and kissed their cheeks for the last time.

Dad took Eliza and me to the airport, then we flew back to Tennessee. Two days later, my grandparents died within a few hours of one another. My aunt said it was the most romantic way they could have gone and said it was just like *The Notebook.* And that's what she told all her family and friends, and herself. Dad was in shock, I think. He stayed for their funeral arrangements. My aunt was already busy telling all the siblings how much money they would receive from the will and who would get what from my grandparents' possessions. No one had time to grieve. She kicked Dad out of her house after the cremation, and he came back to Tennessee seemingly defeated. Everything else over the next few months was blurry. We were up and down with feeding the baby throughout the nights and figuring out parenthood. We slept when we could. Luke remained stressed over his job, and our relationship was rocky, but we parented well together.

I didn't know how to make Dad whole again. It broke my heart to see him that way. I missed my grandparents, too. I was so thankful for the traditions and memories they'd shared yet still found myself wishing to undo everything that my aunt had put them through. My thoughts jumped back and forth from my sweet Eliza and this new stage of motherhood to spending summers jumping off the dock in the bay and my grandmother's laugh. *She never stopped smiling or singing.*

24

Our Little Love

My aunt started calling Dad every day after my grandparents passed. She was harassing him. She demanded he return the guitar that my grandfather had given him several years before. She insisted it to be part of her inheritance. She began messaging me on Facebook about a ring that my grandmother had given me when I was 12 years old. She told my dad she wouldn't allow him to have any of his inheritance if I did not give her that ring. I was disturbed by her messages and realized the only way to get her to stop was to block her. She was causing everyone in the family to turn on each other.

I received messages from my Aunt Amelia and was confused on who to trust in the whirlwind of name calling and finger pointing over my grandmother's ring. I just wanted to be there for Dad and was loyal to him above all else. He had still not seen a doctor to follow up with his defibrillator implant.

Luke continued working the marketing gig, though it was clear he didn't like it there. We talked about hopping in the car and going back west to pick up where we'd first met. We had a baby now, though, and had to figure out a plan of sorts rather than just going on a whim. *Didn't we?*

Dad was enamored with Eliza, and she gave life to his days. They had immediately bonded since the day of her birth; the first time he'd held her there in the hospital room. Eliza was a shining beacon of light in some very dark times.

We took a road trip up to Chicago for Memorial Day weekend to introduce Eliza to her great-grandparents on Luke's side. Everyone was happy to welcome a new baby into the family. Eliza's great-grandfather serenaded her with a song on the guitar while we had lunch. Then, everyone took turns passing her around. My early motherhood instincts had me latching onto her and watching her every move.

A couple weeks after returning home, Luke's grandfather had taken a fall and been admitted into the hospital. He passed away in the coming days, and the world lost another good soul. I'd always remember his smile from across the dinner table the first time I met him, both with barbeque splattered on our lips, when he'd welcomed me into their family with open arms.

Eliza amazed us every day, as we navigated this new space of becoming new parents and grieving the loss of our own grandparents. We were entering as a new generation of parents, a passing of the torch and an uncharted new phase. We relished doing "tummy time" with Eliza. Being a mother was such a joy. Nothing compares to the warmth of your newborn baby laying tummy down on top of your own tummy, a bonding like no other. She was purely sweet and so little. We spent lots of time all hanging out in bed as a new family the days that followed. We sang to her a lot and collected many books to add to her growing collection. Her room was a place of peace and solace during the life transitions that were taking place. It seemed 10 years of life had happened over the last year.

Luke and I would crawl onto the carpeted floor of her nursery room and nap alongside her crib, where she lay. We talked about life and how the last year had flown by. We spoke of possibilities for our future and where we wanted to end up. I had no idea at this point, but we both knew at some point we wanted to raise Eliza out West and teach her to snowboard.

25

Postpartum

I enrolled back into college classes full-time and wanted to make my grandfather's legacy proud, with two more semesters to go. I'd promised. Dad stayed at the condo with Eliza on Tuesdays and Thursdays while I went to school and Luke to work. I started working back at the clinic after a brief maternity leave on Mondays, Wednesdays, and Fridays. Some days, I brought Eliza to work with me to hang out with the girls. They loved her, and we were both welcomed there.

School helped keep my mind busy, while I was still feeling overwhelmed by unwarranted thoughts of Mom. I couldn't seem to escape them. My grandparents had died so suddenly. Dad was grieving and still recovering from his heart attack. *Was I being a good enough mother?* I went to the final checkup at my OBGYN and told her I was having strong thoughts of suicide that I couldn't seem to push away. I was waking up daily with thoughts of ending it all and couldn't understand why. I'd never felt that way before, never been suicidal prior to having a child, and loved being Eliza Mae's mother. I told the doc that I couldn't make the thoughts go away. I vented to her one of my darkest secrets, that I was terrified of inheriting my mother's mental illness and didn't ever want to put that burden on Eliza. And that I had become so obsessed with that possibility during postpartum, it had led to having suicidal thoughts. The doc did a couple verbal and written assessments, then diagnosed me with *Severe Postpartum Depression*. My TennCare insurance was ending soon, and since this would be my last appointment with my doctor, I asked a lot of questions.

She prescribed me Zoloft, and I went home and did a lot of research on the medication. I didn't like taking prescription medication, especially after witnessing my mother's mental health challenges over the years. She'd had terrible withdrawals from the medications doctors prescribed, and I'd watched her mental health blow up after all the pills they'd given her. I didn't know if it was better to take them or to try a natural alternative. And with my insurance ending with no affordable options for healthcare coverage, I would have to stop taking the Zoloft abruptly without having a doctor to guide me through the process. Seeing Mom go through those withdrawals was horrific and left her worse coming out on the other side. Getting outside and exercising always made me feel better, like rigorous hiking, whitewater rafting, and biking, and it all seemed out of reach in our current scenario balancing parenthood, work, and school. I flushed the Zoloft down the toilet in a whirlwind and tried to ignore the intrusive thoughts by staying active.

School helped. I went to the library often to study. When I tried to do my homework at home, I felt trapped in conversations with Dad about my mother. He still wanted us to reconnect amidst everything else we were processing, and I couldn't do it. I was feeling increasingly irritable and still hormonal even after pregnancy. I was in no way ready to confront Mom, let her be around Eliza, or entertain thoughts of her knowing where we lived. It was too much. My favorite time of day was going to bed for the evenings and having tummy time with Eliza before her nighttime feeding routines.

Thanksgiving was around the corner; it had been seven months since I'd given birth, and looking back, I was *depressed*. I felt claustrophobic at our condo. I squeezed in writing my college essays while Eliza napped. I hid in our bedroom to find space. Dad said I needed to visit Mom and let her be around the baby, since she was Eliza's grandmother. And I think it was extra timely for him with my grandparents recently passing. I couldn't seem to escape the thoughts of her mental illness.

Thoughts of Mom crept up my neck, all dark and negative memories now, pulsing through my mind like poison. I couldn't even remember the good times anymore or how we used to be close. It started to feel like she'd always been this way, erratic and filled with spiteful chaos and pretend stories. She had turned into this dark figment in my mind that haunted my home, and I couldn't seem to escape her.

Even on the opposite side of the country, I'd worried about her. Now that I was a mother, I'd just wanted to raise my baby without having to think about fixing or becoming like my own mother. Dad couldn't let it go, couldn't let *her* go. He disapproved of my boundary I'd set with her and maybe didn't accept that my mental strength was dwindling. He wanted me to have a relationship with her so she could be around Eliza, too. He still struggled to accept she was mentally ill and not ever going to change back to her old self. I felt trapped in that condo and needed to get out. I wanted Eliza and me to have our own safe space away from all the chaos.

I invited my old roommates, Gilly and Booker, over the night before Thanksgiving. I needed to clear my head. Dad had been talking about us bringing Eliza over to visit with Mom for the holiday. I became defensive and protective and said, "There is no way in hell I'm taking my child around that man she has living down there." I could feel the walls closing in, as I defended my boundary around introducing Eliza to my mother. I wasn't ready.

I felt the world caving in, shadows expanding over me, as if I was lying in a deep hole suffocated by the darkness. This was postpartum. My house wasn't mine, and I didn't know where to go to breathe. Luke and I argued more often, and I felt so lost from the person I used to be. Maybe it was untreated postpartum depression, or maybe the weight of my inability to accept my mother's mental illness had finally won.

She'd always say, "Millie, I'm trying to get you to laugh," like I was some stiff, stuck-up version of myself. I had felt more carefree growing up, full of laughter and seeking fun during my school years. I remember feeling so light and optimistic about the world back then. I couldn't remember how to laugh around her or how to be myself around her. I was scared of becoming like her. And in that state, it was hard to remember any good.

Gilly showed up at the condo with a bottle of Wild Turkey. I took the first drink I'd had since the week I'd found out about Dad's widowmaker heart attack back in Florida. I took a shot and washed away the thoughts of Mom. A second shot to evaporate the things my aunt did to my father. And a third to ignore that my grandparents had slept an untimely death.

Eliza was asleep upstairs, and Luke had gone to bed after we'd spent most of the week arguing about our future together. It was hard to envision a future together after discovering his group chat of women he fantasized with his friends about. I'd wished he had a bank account for them, too, at that moment.

Dad retreated to his room in the basement. I didn't know who I was anymore. I drank a fourth shot and felt my blood turn warm. My old roommates had no idea that I wasn't drinking to celebrate or be thankful. I was drinking to forget. Drinking to block out my feelings, because they'd gotten too heavy to bare alone. Drinking to feel numb, because that felt easier than the heaviness. I hated Thanksgiving and all holidays since my mammaw had passed away. I'd disliked holidays in general since Dad moved to Florida and since Mom had lost her mind. This time of year, I had been used to spending time alone, hiking in the mountains for half a decade. It had been me and the dogs. I was drinking to escape the condo and to find a place where I didn't have to think about Mom, a place where I could be free.

My old roommates left. I sat there at our dinner table alone in a drunken stupor. A year's worth of worry fled my shoulders, and I screamed. Dad came up the stairs, and Luke came down. "I can't do this anymore!" I yelled. I broke a picture frame that held a picture of mine and Luke's first date from out in the Tetons.

"I can't do it!" I screamed.

"What are you talking about?" asked Dad.

"Millie, calm down," said Luke.

"I'm done!" I said.

It all felt so heavy. I didn't want to become like *her. Eliza would be better off without me,* the postpartum said. Then, it exploded out, all at once. The buildup of tension erupted like a tormented volcano. *I needed advice on how to be a mother and how to get through pregnancy, and she wasn't there. I almost bled to death giving birth, and the last thing I gave a fuck about was bonding an impossible relationship with my mentally ill mother.* All the thoughts were flooding back, and I kept thinking of Mom grabbing me by the throat and slamming me into that wall. *Now, a house of ghosts.* I was so scared of becoming like that. Becoming just like her. Dad tried to calm me down, and *I shoved him away from me into the refrigerator* and lost my vision. When I came to, there was heartbreak in his eyes, but the whiskey had taken over. Eliza was crying upstairs, and Luke went to soothe her.

I locked myself in the bathroom. *It would be best if I was out of everyone's lives,* the whiskey reassured me. I imagined the world better without me in it and wondered if death would be a welcomed retreat to the pain I felt. I stared into the bathroom mirror, thoughts of killing myself overflowing, and came to. *What are you doing, Millie?*

A loud tapping came on the front door of the condo. Dad opened it, and a police officer asked to come into the house. He said someone had reported a loud scream coming from our unit. I stepped out from behind Dad and told the officer it was me. I told him that I hated Thanksgiving and asked him to handcuff me. I told him I had been nothing but trouble to Luke and my father. I told him it was best to remove me from the condo. I *needed* to get out of there. I *wanted* to get out of there. The cop said that he couldn't take me anywhere unless Dad and Luke filed a report. They asked me not to go, but I knew that I couldn't stay there, not like that. I asked the officer if he would take me to the hospital for a voluntary mental evaluation. I told him I felt suicidal. He agreed to take me then. I explained to him that I knew the process very well from time after time ordering mental evals to no avail for my mother, as she'd refused to go.

Luke was hurting. He told me to sleep it off, but I knew I needed help. He didn't understand the pain I felt; *he couldn't.* The pain hurt so deep, I didn't know how to even begin healing. He walked with me to the police car. It all felt like a bad dream but no worse than the ones I'd been having at night of Mom and those sharp-clawed alien demons she fantasized about. I watched Luke's and Dad's faces grow dim with sadness, confusion, and disappointment from the backseat of the cop car. The same looks I had given to Mom in the unmarked white van when they took her away that night at the hospital. They couldn't possibly understand what I was feeling. And still drunk, I knew what I had to do.

I peered from behind a black screen to the front seat wondering if this was how Mom had felt all those times she'd been arrested or involuntarily sent to the hospital.

We arrived at the hospital. The officer walked me in, and the nursing staff put me into a room.

"Why are you here?" the male nurse asked.

"I requested a voluntary mental evaluation," I said.

"It's going to be a couple hours before the mental health professional will arrive, so we are going to take some blood tests," he said.

I hated having blood drawn and half-regretted my choice to be there. Luke showed up half an hour later.

"Why are you doing this?" he asked.

"I have to know," I said.

"Know what?" he asked.

"If I am going to end up like her, Luke. I have know for Eliza," I said.

The nurse came back, said blood tests were good, and we could leave if we wanted.

"I don't want to leave before the exam," I said.

Thoughts of holding Mom hostage in hospitals, as my aunt and I waited for the mental evaluation professionals, flooded my mind. All the times we had to trick her into having mental evaluations, and here I was begging for one, and they were sending me away.

"She threatened to kill herself tonight," Luke told the nurse.

"What? That wasn't on record. You will have to wait here," he said.

The mental health professional showed up and asked Luke to step outside.

"Millie, what happened tonight?" he asked.

"I drank some whiskey, sir, but all the things I said have been on my mind for a while," I told him.

"Do you have a personal history of mental health issues?" he asked.

"My mother is schizophrenic and bipolar," I said.

"So why are *you* here?" he asked.

"I've read that it's genetic, and I don't want to end up like her. I just had my daughter back in April, and since the postpartum depression, I'm so scared that I'm going to lose my mind," I said, crying without refrain.

"I see. Well, let me ask you a few questions," he said.

He asked me my name, the date, and a few other things about family health history. I responded with simple answers.

"You need to go home and get some rest. And stop researching so much. If you were sick like your mother, it would have more than likely happened by now," he said. "The holidays are a rough time for a lot of people."

Filled with guilt, I apologized to my dad and Luke on Thanksgiving Day. I also felt somewhat of a weight off my shoulders with the medical examiner's reassurance and a not-so-healthy way to release all the emotions that had been building. We made a cumbersome turkey, stuffed with melancholy. I held Eliza so tightly at home.

"I think this is rock bottom," I told Luke.

"Well, that means you can only go up from here," he said.

Dad ended up buying a fixer-upper house a few miles away from our condo. He said that it was time for him to move out and figure out what to do with this next chapter of his life. And besides, we would still see him weekly, since he watched Eliza while I was going to school every Tuesday and Thursday.

The semester came to an end. In honor of my grandpa, now up in Heaven, I'd made straight As and was one step closer to completing my first college degree. To celebrate, I took Eliza out to one of my favorite spots on the Nolichucky

River. Right below a familiar rapid under the Chestoa Bridge, she dipped her toes into the Noli for her very first time. It was a special moment in a magical place I had shared growing up with my mother.

26

Closing Time

One night, Luke and I sat down in Eliza's nursery with a notepad and pen. We wrote down all our finances and made a plan to get back out West. We started applying for jobs and researching housing. I had become obsessed with the #VanLife movement of our generation and had been looking up vans for sale on Craigslist. I ran the idea by Luke, and he said it would be a good way to save money and get back out there. Work was really getting to Luke, and he had dreaded going into the office each morning. It was time to look outside of Tennessee, once more. We agreed that if we really wanted to do Van Life, we would have to stick around for another few months to prepare. I only had one semester of school left to get my associate's degree and committed to sign up for classes that following January.

Dad seemed content in his new house and was working on small projects, one at a time. He told Mom where he lived. Eventually, after some time had passed, I'd agreed to meet her at a park in town so she could meet Eliza for the first time. I was nervous and unsure of what to expect. Mom was hearing voices I couldn't hear and couldn't focus on meeting her grandbaby. She was distracted by her visions of a man trapped in a tree at the park, and after about an hour, we left. I wasn't ready.

27

Van Life

We applied often for jobs out West, mainly in the Tetons. We sat down on the floor of the nursery, again, and I made a five-year plan. We talked to our family about our decision to do Van Life. Luke's dad surprisingly told us to go for it. Dad said to follow our hearts, though I did not like the idea of leaving him back in Tennessee.

I spoke with an advisor at school and was set up to graduate that following May. The new year was upon us already, and Luke came home from work one evening with a slip of paper. His boss had let him go. I think he was relieved to not have to work there anymore.

This news gave us motivation to make a change. We had looked at a few vans in person and test drove a couple that seemed promising. They all had their own issues and surprises. Luke posted an ad on Facebook stating that we were looking for a Class B Campervan if anyone had any leads. Later that same day, a lady messaged him about a GMC that she and her husband owned. It sat in their backyard in Erwin and was being used for kayak storage out near the Nolichucky River.

We went to test drive it a few days later. It was a 1986 Class B Vandura. The lady's father had bought the van brand new back in its prime from a dealer in New York, and it barely had any signs of rust. The odometer rested at 33,000 miles. The engine started up strong as we drove it around town. She ran like a noble steed or seemed to, at least. The interior was in great condition and put off major '70s vibes with shag brown everything. It was like the van-version of the old farmhouse I'd grown up in. There were more amenities than we'd ever need: a fridge, sink, pull-out bed, swivel chair, top bunk, toilet, and shower/bath combo. We inquired about the asking price. They wouldn't take less than $4,200. We only had $2,500 cash saved up and told them we'd have to hold off two weeks until we got our tax returns. They said to keep in touch.

28

Tying Up Loose Ends

School started, and all I could think about was that van. Luke qualified for unemployment after the layoff. If we wanted the van, we'd have to sacrifice renting the condo at $950 a month, so we put in our 30 days' notice and began moving boxes over to Dad's house. He said we could stay in a room there for as long as we needed and was happy to have Eliza so close. It was only 15 minutes away from school, and Dad welcomed us without hesitation. I welcomed thoughts of getting back *on the road*. I was mesmerized by it, and though I loved school, I fantasized about living in the van and traveling with Eliza every day that semester.

Our tax returns came in. After another test drive, we came back to Dad's with a brown high-top van. We took Eliza into it and let her play on the top bunk that would be remodeled into her own space. There were still a few renovations the van needed before she'd be road ready. Sweet Brown, I called her, needed an alternator and a battery first thing. And that was only the beginning. We ripped out the brown musty carpet and replaced it with vinyl flooring so that it would be easier to clean and sweep dog hair. We built Eliza a wooden gate and attached it to the base of her bunk to keep her from rolling out. Luke found two new lawn chair cushions that fit perfectly together as her bunk mattress. After thinking about it for a few days, we decided to remove the toilet. It would save time and space. We'd be around bathrooms often enough along highways or in the woods while camping.

We took the van out to the local DMV to get plates, and it was official. We were given the keys to our first home (on wheels).

May was creeping up on us, and the carburetor was causing issues. A few kicks and bangs later, the van was starting up and running on mere gasoline and prayers. I traced the dogs' paw prints and Eliza's hand on the side of the van and signed their names: Luna, Bosco, and Eliza Mae. Dad helped us put a fresh coat of wax on the van, and she was road ready.

I graduated Summa Cum Laude the second week of May, obtaining my associate's degree from a small community college in rural Appalachia. Mom, Dad, Luke, and Eliza came to my graduation to celebrate, and it filled my heart to see the four of them sitting there in the stands together. *This one's for you, Grandpa,* I thought when walking up to get my diploma.

I got a wild hair and told Luke and Dad to take Eliza home, and I would ride back to Dad's house with Mom. She was having a good day that day, and I wanted to spend some time with her before we hit the road again. She had always cheered me on from the basketball stands in elementary school, and I was thankful she'd made it out to my first college graduation.

We rode in her car with the windows down, and I told her I loved her so much. I told her it meant the world to me that she had shown up that day and that we'd be leaving the following morning to head West, for good. *And that I would miss her.*

Morning came. Tears flooded down my cheeks in the shower, as I dreaded leaving my parents in Tennessee. And it was time to go. Sarah stopped by Dad's house to wish us well on our journey and hug her godchild. Luke took a few pics of us all in front of the van for the scrapbook.

I hugged Dad, sobbing to no end, and he hugged me, Luke, and kissed Eliza on each cheek. It was a new day. Luke started up the engine and backed down Dad's driveway. I did the "endless wave" all the way down his street until we were out of sight. Then, with my gaze set forward, I exhaled, happy to be back *on the road.*

"There was nowhere to go but everywhere,
so just keep on rolling under the stars."
— JACK KEROUAC, ON THE ROAD

RIVERS AND ROADS

MILLIE'S ROAD TRIP SOUNDTRACK

1. "Rivers and Roads" by The Head and the Heart
2. "(Sittin' on) The Dock of the Bay" by Otis Redding
3. "West Coast" by Lana Del Rey
4. "Going to California" by Led Zeppelin
5. "Bad Karma" by Axel Thesleff
6. "California" by Phantom Planet
7. "Coming Home" by Leon Bridges
8. "Pacific Coast Highway" by The Hip Abduction with Trevor Hall
9. "San Francisco (Be Sure to Wear Some Flowers in Your Hair)" by Scott McKenzie
10. "All Apologies" by Nirvana
11. "Old Pine" by Ben Howard
12. "The Traveling Song" by The Avett Brothers
13. "American Girl" by Tom Petty and the Heartbreakers
14. "Here's to Now" by Ugly Casanova
15. "Under the Bridge" by Red Hot Chili Peppers
16. "Don't Panic" by Coldplay
17. "Growing Up" by Run River North
18. "And We Danced" by The Hooters
19. "Don't Wait for Me" by Josh Garrels
20. "Death and All His Friends" by Coldplay

21. "Dashboard" by Modest Mouse

22. "Blame It on the Tetons" by Modest Mouse

23. "Hey Mami (Big Wild Remix)" by Sylvan Esso

24. "Coffee" by Sylvan Esso

25. "Adventure of a Lifetime" by Coldplay

26. "Wolf" by Sylvan Esso

27. "Landslide" by Fleetwood Mac

28. "You Are Your Mother's Child" by Conor Oberst

29. "One Headlight" by The Wallflowers

30. "Closing Time" by Semisonic

LET THE WILD IN

By Alicia M. Bynum

Let the wilderness seep inside you
Like a fresh whiff of honeysuckle

Let it coarse through your veins
Like nature's heroin

Let it become you as you breathe each precious breath
Until you can no longer stand
How Feral
Your soul has accepted
Your very existence

Mary called it one, wild and precious
For it is
And you can no longer deny
The Wild
In which
You seek to hide

Embrace and become
Like the wolves howl and the monkeys scream
Become like them, as you are
And deny not
The blood in which you were brought

Come one, come wild
Shatter all which tried
To stop you from becoming
That which you've always been
Let the wild in

SHE

By Alicia M. Bynum

Who is this girl
Weathered by the world
She stands with her shoulders broad,
And boundaries made of stone
Won't you look at her,
Look at how she's grown
Tides pull with crumbling weight,
Yet she stands tall
With a piercing gaze
Eyes so sharp,
They'd shatter an unspoken lie
A smell for cruel intentions,
And a heart that won't die

Who is this girl
Have you seen her
Hands that could suppress an army,
Or nurture a newborn baby
Who is she
Why has she come,
Or maybe she never left
Growing through the tests of time,
Walking softly among frozen pines

That girl is you
That girl is me
She is us,
We
Our mothers and grandmothers
Our daughters
She

If you or a loved one has experienced mental health or substance abuse challenges, know that you are not alone and there are resources available. If you're interested in taking action by learning how to have challenging and meaningful conversations, please consider becoming Mental Health First Aid certified at Mentalhealthfirstaid.org.

ACKNOWLEDGMENTS

A special note of gratitude to Jan-Carol Publishing, a local publisher based in East Tennessee, for publishing my first novel. And to my dog, Dobby, who spent countless hours curled up in a ball by my feet while I poured out words on the keyboard.

ABOUT THE AUTHOR

ALICIA M. BYNUM is a first-time author of the novel *Rivers and Roads*. She enjoys spending time with her family, exploring the great outdoors, writing, reading, and painting. She's an advocate for protecting public lands, expanding mental health care access across the Appalachian region, and researching connections between nature and wellbeing. Alicia currently resides in rural Appalachia with her daughter, partner, dog, and their two cats. Learn more at Aliciabynum.com.